The Lady and the Barrister

Ruth A.
Casie

The Lady and the Barrister

Timeless Scribes
Publishing

Timeless Scribes Publishing LLC

Digital ISBN-13: 978-1-945679-89-6
Print ISBN-13: 978-1-945679-90-2

Editor: The Editing Hall – Chris Hall

Cover Artist: Wicked Smart Designs

This edition published by arrangement with Timeless Scribes Publishing LLC.

www.TimelessScribes.com

Also by Ruth A. Casie

Regency Romance
THE LADIES OF SOMMER-BY-THE-SEA
The Lady and Her Quill
The Lady and the Spy
The Lady and her Duke
RETURN TO THE LADIES OF SOMMER-BY-THE-SEA
The Lady and the Barrister

Fantasy Romance
THE STELTON LEGACY
The Guardian's Witch
The Highlander's English Woman
The Maxwell Ghost

Crossover Series - Pirate Romance
PIRATES OF BRITANNIA
Donald (Sons of Sagamore)
Hugh (Sons of Sagamore)
Graham (Sons of Sagamore)
The Pirate's Jewel
The Pirate's Redemption

Time Travel Romance
THE DRUID KNIGHT SERIES
Knight of Runes
Knight of Rapture
The Red Slippers — A Short Story
The Druid Knight Tale I — A Short Story—Expanded
The Druid Knight Tale II — A Short Story

Also by Ruth A. Casie

Contemporary Novellas
HAVENPORT
Happily Ever After
The Witching Hour
Never Say Never
Echoes of Betrayal
How to Marry a Stuart Brother
Heart of the Matter

Prologue

The last time Lady Marianna Ravencroft sat with Captain Fraser Castleton, Retd, for any length of time, was the summer of 1809, five years ago when he joined her for tea. They sat in her garden at Raven Hall and talked for hours.

Well, he talked. She listened. They knew each other growing up and enjoyed each other's company. It didn't take long before they once again teased each other, sliding back into that comfortable place.

Anna, a soft smile on her lips, couldn't keep from looking at him. Not to stare, but to make sure he was really there. His natural open presence was welcoming. There was still a hint of his wild warrior ways. Life's design had taught him to harness that energy to transform him into a secure, confident, compassionate man. He was ruggedly handsome. Perhaps that was the lasting effect of his wild days. She chuckled to herself.

She took a deeper look and relented. He was physically handsome with his dark wavy hair just a bit too long, his well-trimmed beard, his blue green eyes just a bit too bright, and a devastating smile that always curled her toes. She let out a breath and tried to relax said toes.

Their time together was more than pleasant, although she did notice there was one part of his life he would not divulge. He skirted around the horrors he experienced during his five years in the service until finally he seemed to run out of words. The only ones left were about the war. About his brother, Lucian.

The silence went on for several agonizing minutes. Mrs. Cutler, Ravencroft's housekeeper, brought a plate of tarts and ginger biscuits along with a pot of tea. Still, he said nothing. Anna poured his tea and fortified it with a splash of her father's brandy. His chest heaved, and he let the air out slowly. His face turned into a mask of pain, hurt, anger, and acceptance all rolled into one.

"I've buried Lucian's death deep. Every time I think I can talk about it…" He stared at his shaking hands then at her.

"When you want to talk, I'm here to listen." Anna covered his hands with her own, a surprising warmth spread through her.

His breathing was ragged as he struggled for control.

"You have no idea. Imagine the worst thing you can think of. That is not half as bad as what I observed." He paused. "What I had to do. Things I want to tell you but cannot." His voice was barely a whisper.

Oh, but she did have some insight. He wasn't aware that she and her friend Lady Harriet Manning had helped soldiers who returned from the war. Hattie was a beautiful person inside and out. On the outside, she had a trim frame, fine features, and expressive amber eyes. Her hair, when not neatly gathered in a knot at the base of her neck, was long and thick. It was the most interesting shade of a reddish brown, the color of fine burgundy.

On the inside, Hattie was a compassionate caregiver. Medically trained by her father, the Earl Manning and a renowned physician, Hattie in turn taught Anna what to do. Together, they nursed men physically and mentally. Each man was a survivor, a hero, not a victim of Napoleon and his war.

For now, she remained quiet. Castleton needed to talk.

"The brutality. What one man is capable of doing to another. A man you never met. A man just as scared as you." Castleton said nothing for a few minutes. "That was four years ago, and to me, it was yesterday."

What went on in his head? From his grimace, she suspected he continued to fight an internal battle. She wanted to put her arms around him and give him her strength, but that would do more harm than good. Instead, she waited and listened.

"Lucian and I served together. We were never far from each other. Barrington sent us to assist Vice-Admiral Nelson." He closed his eyes.

Anna schooled herself not to react, but dear God, he was back in the thick of it all, on the *HMS Victory*.

"Captain Hardy, Lucian, and I were on Victory's deck with the Vice-Admiral as he paced the quarterdeck with the battle waging around us. A multitude of ordnance exploded in quick succession, creating an echo so painful it felt as if your head was about to burst.

"With each explosion came the sound of splintering wood, the crash of debris into the water or onto the deck. But worse were the screams and groans of the wounded men. We strained to hear our orders over the din."

Anna sat numb. For her, he painted vivid, terrible pictures. They were more horrendous for Castleton. Now, months later, he was back in the middle of it, seeing the explosions, smelling the gunpowder, and hearing the screams. Reliving it again, as if once wasn't enough.

"In the tumult, no one heard the blast of a single rifle, but a single shot it was. Fired from the mizzen of the French ship *Redoubtable*. The shot hit Nelson in his left shoulder. He collapsed at my feet. I went to his aid, but he wouldn't let me carry him. Instead, I helped him to his feet and gave him my shoulder.

"Before I went below deck, I saw Lucian run to the gunwale with his rifle raised. He got his shot off. The assassin did as well. I watched the man fall from the mizzen. Hardy urged me to take Nelson below. I didn't know the assassin's shot had been true, that he shot Lucian in his chest."

The pain in his eyes tore at her, but she couldn't do or say anything to comfort him. *Let him talk.*

"While I helped Nelson, my brother, my twin brother lay dying above me." He stared into the garden. "I didn't sit with him. Help him. Ease his way. I didn't… say good-bye." His words trailed off. Silent for several minutes, at last he took a deep breath. "When I found him, I cradled him in my arms, and I vowed with all my heart that I would finish his mission and care for those he held dear." He stared at her with watery eyes. "And cried."

Anna couldn't sit still a moment longer. She knelt next to his chair, put her arm around him, and held him close.

They sat without speaking, her throat knotted and hot with grief. She couldn't say anything if she wanted to. And if she did speak, what would she say? She was sorry for his loss? She understood how he felt? All empty words that held little meaning and meant less.

Anna gently placed her hand over his.

Castleton turned over his hand and intertwined his fingers with hers. After what seemed like hours, he gazed at her. Raw hurt glittered in his eyes. He gently squeezed her hand before he released her.

She went back to her seat.

"What will you do now?" She might as well finish what she started even though his answer was not what she wanted to hear. She removed the last tart from the serving dish and put it on his plate.

Mrs. Cutler brought in a fresh pot of tea and heated Castleton's cup.

"Thank you, Mrs. Cutler." One corner of his mouth pulled into a smile. "I missed your tarts."

"At least now you're not pilfering them and running from my kitchen. I'm too old to run after you with my rolling pin." The housekeeper shook her head.

There was a faint gleam of humor in his eyes, and his mouth curved into an unconscious smile. Anna found his smile catching.

"You're a wonderful and generous woman." Castleton's sincerity took the woman by surprise.

"It was all a hoax. I can tell you now. I made extra tarts for you and your friends."

"But you waved your rolling pin—" His voice rose in feigned surprise.

"And laughed as you grabbed the tarts and ran away. My own lads did the same. I remember the day one of the boys from the village pushed your brother, and he dropped his prize into the pond. You gave him yours and metered out justice, making the unruly boys work off their debt. It was no surprise to me that you became a barrister."

"Ah, that was why a lone tart remained on the cooling rack when I came by the kitchen. You nodded toward the tart and turned your back." A faraway, amused look filled his eyes as he licked his lips.

"I think that was the most delicious tart I ever ate."

"I wouldn't let you go hungry." Mrs. Cutler nodded and withdrew. The misty look on the woman's face caught Anna by surprise.

"I understand now. You're here for Mrs. Cutler's tarts." Anna teased him as she did when they were younger.

"I missed you too, Anna. Unfortunately, I won't be here long. I return to London in the morning. I've decided I must pick up where I left off at the Inns of Court."

She settled back in her chair, disappointed.

"We must write, and you have to plan to visit when you're in London."

"If you are leaving so soon, then I had best give you your present." Anna nodded to the footman who stood by the door.

"Present? What for?" There may have been a trace of denial in his voice, but the childlike expectation of a gift lit up his face.

A furry brown and black ball with a splash of white snorted and happily bounded toward her. The pup made a stop at Castleton's feet, then sat at attention, her eyes bright and her tongue out.

"Fraser Castleton, let me introduce you to Kaiah. She's from a unique breed of herding dogs. She can keep you company on your walks, even in London. You will be the talk of Hyde Park."

Kaiah nuzzled his hand.

"I've tried to teach her proper manners, but she shamelessly craves attention."

He ruffled Kaiah's silky coat.

"Does she play fetch?" He was still stroking her coat.

Anna nodded to Kaiah. The dog trotted off to the garden and brought back a stick. She sat in front of Castleton, put down the toy, and eagerly waited.

They spent the next several minutes with the pup racing in the garden.

Castleton's smile set her at ease. If only she could make him smile that way.

"I've decided to devote myself to my profession." He kept tossing a stick for Kaiah to retrieve.

"That's an admirable goal."

"Aunt Adelaide would have me believe that a well-established profession is followed by a well-established family. I hate to disappoint her, but I see no family in my future."

"No family?" Everyone wanted a family. Family was loving and supporting one another. She couldn't imagine life without her family, and she looked forward to having one of her own. Where was the man who moments ago teased, challenged, and laughed? She had always known there was something special about him, something special between them.

"Every one of us dies. I will never put anyone I love through that hell." There was a finality in his words, in his stance, in his face. He silently pleaded with her to understand.

She didn't have an answer for him.

He stood in the garden playing with Kaiah, but to Anna, he was already gone, and there was nothing she could do to change his mind or bring him back.

He and Kaiah departed the next day. He did come back to Sommer-by-the-Sea to see his Aunt Adelaide, the Duchess of Willbury every so often, but their paths went in different directions.

Chapter One

September 7, 1814
Sommer-by-the-Sea

"Today, of all days." The mumbled words fell from Lady Anna's lips. As soon as they were out, she regretted them and slowed her steps. What was she thinking? Tea was not an imposition. She took a calming breath and continued on. Today, of all days, was a fine day for a cup of tea with her close friend.

"Lady Anna."

Startled, she came to a halt as she peered to see who called her. The tall slender proprietor of the circulating library stood in front of her. His pleasing manner and open face made him easy to talk to. Once you started him on a topic, he would site book titles and, at times, recite passages. His knowledge was vast, which could be why he was also a school master at the Barrow School for Young Men in Newcastle. He touched the brim of his hat.

"Mr. Miller." She acknowledged his greeting with a nod.

"I have to tell you how much I enjoyed the Sommer-by-the-Sea Foundation Gala last evening. Everyone will be talking about it all during and after the London Season."

Anna had planned that event for months. Every detail had to be perfect. And in the end, it was, at least to those who attended.

"I'm glad you enjoyed the evening. The Foundation raised a considerable amount of money. There will be coal in stoves and food for the poor this winter."

"It was for a good cause. The theme, I knew it was the four seasons, but the room, the food. I have no words to describe the event. How do you do it? Each event you create is better than the last. I'm surprised Queen Charlotte hasn't swept you away to London."

Anna beamed with pride. If only Mr. Miller knew the near catastrophes she had to manage behind the scenes. The overcooked food, the wilted flowers, and the carved blocks of ice melting far faster than she anticipated.

"Lady Alicia's new book arrived at the library yesterday. I'll put one aside for you."

"You have my gratitude. I would be cross with myself if I didn't read her book. She would be cross if I didn't read it. When we were studying at the seminary together, she would read her stories to us. I always thought they were wonderful. I'm proud and excited for her success. I'll stop by for it later today."

"You have set expectations for your next event. Everyone will want to attend." He touched the edge of his hat in salute and went on his way.

He would be excited. Her next event was at his circulating library.

As she crossed Westmore Commons, an autumn breeze pulled at her bonnet, ruffled her skirt, and blew open the bottom of her pelisse. The aroma of fresh-baked Russian biscuits in the air drew her toward the tearoom. The work she was doing for two other events would simply have to wait. She took a deep breath. Tea and biscuits. Yes, today of all days.

Anna hurried down King's Way. She was among a cadre of graduates from Mrs. Honoria Bainbridge's elite Sommer-by-the-Sea Female Seminary who stayed close to the headmistress joining her for tea. Prospective students didn't apply to the seminary. Mrs. Bainbridge personally chose each young woman. Some are born sisters, others find each other. For these smart progressive women of The Ladies of Sommer-by-the-Sea, their eternal bond couldn't have been stronger if it were forged in steel.

There wasn't any time to revel in last night's success, although even she admitted the results pleased her.

"Lady Marianna." A gentleman, attending last night's gala, acknowledged her as she passed.

"Mr. Clark," she nodded in reply. If she remembered correctly, he made a very generous donation.

No, she couldn't spend time dwelling on the gala. The library event was in ten days, and the Harvest Ball was a week after. The campaign reception for her distant cousin Richard was a quick ten days after that.

She entered the busy tearoom and peered across the neat rows of tables, each dressed in a crisp white linen cloth with a lace overlay. Small vases filled with crocus, dahlias, pansies, and goldenrod added a bright autumn touch to the room. She spied Mrs. Bainbridge and Tatiana Chernovsky, the proprietor of the tearoom, seated by the far window.

Mrs. Bainbridge was a woman of virtue, character, learning, and good breeding. A widow, she forged a highly sought-after female seminary that nurtured and developed women who were assets to their families and society. Her charges graduated with not only scholastic knowledge, but a good sense of themselves and how to manage in the world.

An attractive woman in her mid-thirties, Mrs. Bainbridge was fashionable and elegant. Today she wore a verditer-blue silk dress with a matching pelisse. Her long auburn hair streaked with gold was tucked into her bonnet. Soft spoken and intelligent, Anna knew from firsthand experience that the headmistress could be a woman one wouldn't want to cross.

Tanya was a contemporary of Mrs. Bainbridge. With the Barringtons' assistance, the recently widowed Tanya left St. Petersburg and established residency in Sommer-by-the-Sea. She reopened the shuttered tearoom, giving it an added, subtle Russian flare and superb ginger cookies.

Her playful tea readings, that were often mysteriously accurate, contrasted with the formal aristocrat who kept her heritage alive. Her plaited auburn hair was topped off with an obruch. On Tanya it looks like a princess's crown rather than a decorated Russian headband.

Anna made her way to their table.

"I hope I didn't keep you waiting." Anna took a seat next to Tanya, removed her gloves, and placed them in her reticule.

"Not at all. Mrs. Bainbridge and I were reveling in last night's success. I admire that, in lieu of payment, you arrange for those using your service to donate the amount to charity. And she told me you are planning Mr. Younge's campaign reception." Tanya poured Anna a cup of tea and added a splash of milk. "I knew, of course. Mrs. Cutler placed an order for biscuits for the event."

"Serving biscuits from your tearoom is the touch that will ensure he wins the election." She was glad her housekeeper had placed the order.

"Tell me about this cousin of yours."

She didn't expect her involvement in the election would be the first issue discussed. It was no more than she did when the Lord Mayor ran for re-election.

"Richard is campaigning for a seat in the House of Commons soon to be vacated by his father. His reception is a small event for everyone to meet him."

"I'm surprised he wants any part of politics." Mrs. Bainbridge freshened her cup with a splash of hot water. "His somewhat irresponsible youth was the bellwether of a disappointing manhood. He's had several jobs but never remained employed for more than six months at any of them. According to the article in the Sommer Sentinel, while it was kind to him, it pointed out the man never showed any interest in politics."

"In his defense, I lost touch with his branch of the family when they moved away some seven, almost eight years ago. Perhaps he's matured." She turned to Tanya. "Please pass the biscuits."

"Has he changed since you last saw him?" Mrs. Bainbridge had a note of doubt in her voice.

"He is more outgoing and cordial than I remember. I think feisty is how I would have described him when we were young, but now he is…"

"Mature," Mrs. Bainbridge added. "One can hope he's grown to be more like his father, Francis."

"Yes, and likable. I have the reception in hand. Although I will tell you, I check, double-check, and triple-check to make certain everything will run close to perfection." Anna took a breath.

"Your events are always wonderful. This one will be, too. Now, if you'll excuse me, I must get back to the kitchen." Tanya stood and made her way to the front of the shop.

Anna sipped her tea.

"Is that better?" Mrs. Bainbridge looked on with a knowing smile on her lips.

"Richard Younge has no idea how to put together an event."

"Does any man?" The headmistress sipped her tea.

"No, I'm used to producing and controlling my events once my services are secured. Richard can be irritating at times. His priorities are not aligned with mine. I know this event is important to him, but I cannot proceed without a guest list and knowing where the event is to be held." She held up her hand to ward off Mrs. Bainbridge's words. "I know you warned me."

"I didn't say a word." Mrs. Bainbridge looked away. Anna tried to determine if the headmistress gloated over her admission.

"You didn't have to." There was no way she could remain angry. Once again, the woman was correct.

"He's quick to tell me he has the votes needed to win, especially since he is unopposed. He thinks this one reception will give him all the funds he needs. Well, he has much to learn. But enough about Mr. Younge. Let's enjoy our tea." Anna took another sip and bite of biscuit.

"You've been so busy. I missed spending time with you." Mrs. Bainbridge leaned forward and gently squeezed her arm. "We've all missed you. I was determined to take tea with you before you joined your parents."

Anna replaced the teacup on the saucer, her back as stiff as Mrs. Cutler's ironing board. "I have no plans to join them. They're in Newcastle visiting family before they're off to London."

"Oh? The Season begins in late October." Mrs. Bainbridge's smile remained gentle and pleasant.

"I can't attend this year. I have too much to do." She busied herself wiping the crumbs off the table, into her hand, and putting them on the saucer. The thought of another Season gave Anna hives. The embarrassment of two Seasons was quite enough.

Well, that wasn't the entire truth. The Ravenscroft name brought out the rogues of every size, shape, and age. They graced her with a proposal in exchange for access to her family money. A shiver ran across her back thinking of the ordeal.

Sitting on the sideline while one by one the other girls became betrothed and she… Anna let out a deep breath. And she was not. Too keen were the memories of her humiliation and disappointment that slammed into her chest. She didn't deny those women their excitement and their good fortune. However, it was difficult to be excited for them when any hope of a loving marriage and a house filled with children were beyond her reach. No, she would not change her priorities. She demanded a match with a man who supported her independent ways. No, she would not have a third Season. She would not fail again.

"Anna, you haven't listened to a word I said."

She blinked and came back to the moment. "I'm sorry. I didn't mean to be rude. My mind was elsewhere. Please repeat your question."

"Tell me more about the reception." Mrs. Bainbridge warmed her own tea and held the pot over Anna's cup.

"Yes, thank you."

The headmistress poured for her.

"He asked for my help with a small reception. In discussing the event with him, he mentioned the duchess had favored him for the position." She paused, thinking about the woman who was the epitome of creating a gracious event. Anna learned her skills from observing the best women she knew, her mother and Adelaide, the Duchess of Willbury.

The duchess had been a slip of a woman, but powerful. She'd had a quick wit, a gracious presence, and was a good judge of people. She would fight you politely on an issue, then laugh heartily at your jokes.

"I still find it difficult to believe that she's passed on. I took on the task in her memory."

"That is generous of you, but the election is over by the first week in November. Even if you are delayed several weeks afterward the reception, I see no harm in beginning the Season fashionably late."

This wasn't the first time Anna had been a target of Mrs. Bainbridge's directness. The discomforting thought had her shifting in her chair and glancing out the window.

Mrs. Bainbridge leaned across the table and patted her hand. "Forgive me. I am being rude and thoughtless. You're the judge of what is best for you."

Mrs. Bainbridge and Mrs. Cutler had warned her not to be so generous with her time. More than the woman's directness, Anna suspected she had been found out.

Working on the library event and Harvest Ball provided her with an excuse to remain in Sommer-by-the-Sea. Planning Richard's event in early October was preferable to another Season in London and results she could not control.

Rather than being the center of attention at events where she controlled nothing, she decided to be the event hostess where she controlled everything.

It was a good plan, so far. Her charity work was doing well. The charities she supported were thrilled and the personal satisfaction was gratifying. She was proving to be good at what she did. But a match? Or worse, an arrangement? Never.

Thank goodness Mama understood. With her parents' support, she remained at Raven Hall, where she could develop her business. Her mother, the Countess of Haworth, stipulated she stay within the confines and expectations of society and that Mrs. Cutler, the Raven Hall housekeeper, be her chaperone. Anna gladly agreed to the conditions.

Anna didn't know life without Martha Lockhart Cutler. The housekeeper was a permanent fixture in the household. Her story, similar to many others, could be viewed as a sad one, but the resilient woman would never let that happen. A society patron, her father passed away, leaving her alone and deep in debt. Her only alternative was to sell off all she had to pay his financial obligations.

Anna's mother hired Martha to fill the housekeeper position. She was brought up on how to run a house with a stern but gentle touch. The woman worked as hard as the staff. Anna observed and emulated her elegant movement. Several years later, Martha married Mr. Phillip Cutler, the Ravencroft butler. Mrs. Cutler was a gem and quickly became more of an older sister than hired staff. It was a unique relationship.

"I'm grateful for your concern. Really, I am." Anna reached across the table and grasped Mrs. Bainbridge's hand. "I feel much like a duke who is pursued by mothers looking for matches for daughters."

Anna removed her hand, sat up straight, and busied herself with her serviette. "It's amazing what the Ravencroft name and fortune brings out in men. You have no need to worry. I will not be any less than I am. I don't need wealth or even a handsome man to know my self-worth. I want a partner with integrity, compassion, and especially one who is not afraid of a woman with ability and a good mind. I have met men who, on the surface, appear to fit my ideal in almost every way. However, so far, each gentleman has failed in the one non-negotiable value."

"Point well taken. I wouldn't expect any less for you. I wouldn't for myself. And as for your cousin's reception, if I can assist in any way—"

"It is a relief to know I can call upon you. At the moment, my biggest challenge is getting Richard to finalize his guest list and tell me where the reception is to be held." She folded her serviette and placed it on the table.

"I met Mr. Miller on my way here. The copies of Alicia's new book arrived. She is scheduled to be the guest author at next month's reading, and I want to read her book."

"How fortunate. I'm to meet Barrington at the library. We can walk over there together."

Chapter Two

A gust of wind sent dried leaves scurrying along the lane. Small whirlwinds had the leaves chasing one another before the next gust came along and sent them flying in a different direction. In the distance, the masts tipping and canting in the harbor poked over the rooftops of the buildings surrounding the square.

Fraser Castleton, now hailed as the Duke of Willbury though he rejected that title, walked through Westmore Commons, the village square. The heartbeat of the northeastern coastal village pulsed with familiarity, life, and energy. To him it was a welcome relief from London.

He wove his way around the late morning crowd and the marketplace stalls as he came through the square. Children ran after one another playing tag. The aroma of fresh bread had the baker's stall filled with eager buyers. Flowers, trinkets, and kitchen wares filled other stalls. The vibrant village nestled on the rugged northeast coast of England hadn't changed in ten years.

Here, the world did not focus on the *ton* and its goings on. No, the bustling country village centered around the lives of its residents, a fine cross-section of the people of the time. Business flourished and gossip thrived, and unlike London, here the streets were filled with the scent of clean sea air. He took a deep breath and got a whiff of cinnamon and sugar. Like a lad, his mouth watered. The tearoom was nearby.

"Willbury. I say, Willbury."

He walked on.

"Castleton, is that you?"

He lifted his head and scanned the crowd to locate who hailed him. A broad smile brightened his face as he spotted his old friend making his way through the knot of people.

"Barrington. I was on my way to say hello." They stood in the crossroads of two heavily trafficked lanes. The two men stood like boulders in the middle of a fast-flowing stream that required the people to detour around them.

"Sommer-by-the-Sea is getting more like London." Castleton observed the people swirling around them.

"Never. Never that bad. You and I have chosen to plant ourselves in the middle of a busy intersection. Let's move to the side and let them pass." Lord Reese Barrington turned and, leaning heavily on his cane, came to an abrupt stop to avoid colliding with a woman. He tipped his hat. "Good day, Mrs. Collins."

The woman smiled and hurried along.

"This way." Barrington motioned to the right. "How long have you been in Sommer-by-the-Sea?"

"I arrived the night before last." Castleton noted as they threaded through the flow of people that Barrington's limp was more pronounced than usual. His friend leaned heavily on his cane. He kept his tongue behind his teeth, well aware his friend would ask for assistance should he need it.

Barrington's bearing spoke of command and control. Fair and just, he was a protector. Every man in their troop knew it. He was the first one in battle and the last to return to the base. He understood what his men went through because he was at their side.

Severely wounded in action, he worked hard to walk again and even harder to keep his mental strength. He came out the other side with only a limp and a few scars. The worst was across his cheek. His valet cleverly hid it with a well-trimmed beard. His jet black hair was now salt and pepper, but his Nordic blue eyes remained sharp and assessing. Whether in uniform or dressed for a ball, he wore a subdued but commanding air of self-confidence.

It was an offhand remark made by Judge Scofield that had provided Barrington with some needed direction. Several of the men who reported to Barrington were with him at Barrington Hall when the judge visited.

It was after several glasses of whiskey that the discussion turned to smugglers in the area and the lack of a town militia. Bamburgh Castle, where the area militia was stationed, was too far away to respond in a timely fashion. The judge told the men he needed a local militia. One by one, they offered their services as long as Barrington was their commander. And the deal was sealed.

Castleton paused in front of the circulating library and studied the building's façade. The Miller Circulating Library was in a modest-size building. Two oversize plate glass windows with muntins dividing the sash into square panes were on either side of the entrance. Barrington opened the door, setting off the small silver bell attached at the top. The tinkling announced their arrival.

Castleton removed his hat and cast an eye over the familiar space. Shelves and cases overflowing with books covered every wall. Two long desks flanked the room where patrons picked up and brought back their selections. Several sizable tables scattered around the room contained more books.

Mr. and Mrs. Miller's establishment was no different than London's circulating libraries. Fashionable ladies sat in chairs scattered throughout the rooms. Even in this remote village, the ladies were here to see and be seen.

"I wish I had known you arrived. I would have come around for you to join us at last night's Foundation Gala," Barrington said, a warm smile in his voice. "It was a marvelous success."

"That's quite all right. I wanted to get settled in."

"Or to spend time with that beast of a dog of yours. I'm sure Kaiah was glad to have you home."

Barrington led the way to one of the vacant conversation areas in an alcove tucked away from the patrons.

"I am sorry for your loss. Lady Adelaide was a wonderful woman. You have my sincere condolences. Your great-aunt was a down-to-earth and progressive woman with a wicked sense of humor. She will be sorely missed."

"I appreciate your kind words. Aunt Adelaide was a great woman in many ways. She had been ill, but her death was unexpected. Kaiah's barking woke everyone up. But by the time they reached her, there was nothing that could be done. It's difficult to believe she is gone. We were close, but I never expected…" Castleton's voice faded. The pain of his loss was a heavy one.

He let out a slight chuckle as he shook his head. "I still find it strange that the estate and title are mine. I was so far down the line of succession. I hadn't realized that I was the lone survivor."

"Fraser Castleton, the 8th Duke of Willbury. It suits you. I suppose I should be addressing you as Willbury, or do you prefer Your Grace?" Barrington humbly nodded.

"Don't be silly. I am still the same Fraser that spent summers with

Aunt Addie at The Willow and rode to your family's Sommer Chase to spend the day with you and your brother Edward. I love The Willow. I never imagined one day it would be mine."

"My friend, you are the same person with a new responsibility, including a new name. Willbury. It's a good solid name, and one you should be proud to bear. You'll get used to it."

He looked at his former commander. Barrington was correct, of course. Fraser prided himself on never shirking his responsibilities, and now was not the time to start, even if it meant a new name.

"Now, we must celebrate." Barrington leaned forward in his chair. "I am having a small soiree tomorrow evening at my home. You remember Peter Simms and Simon Watts from the regiment. At the request of Judge Scofield, they're the village's volunteer militia. They are attending with their wives, as is Judge Scofield. You must come along."

"Where are you both going?" Mrs. Bainbridge came up and stood by Barrington's chair.

Both men sprang to their feet.

"Honoria, my dear. Let me reintroduce you to the Duke of Willbury. Tell him that he must join us tomorrow evening so we can celebrate his ascension into the ranks of the aristocracy and give him an opportunity to meet his neighbors."

"Mrs. Bainbridge, it is always a pleasure to see you." Castleton tilted his head and gave her a sincere appreciative nod.

"Thank you, Your Grace."

"Please, just Willbury or Fraser." The heat began to creep up his neck. There was no escaping it, he was Willbury. It felt odd, losing a piece of himself while taking on another identity.

"As you like, Willbury. Lord Reese is right. Joining us tomorrow would go far in getting you reacquainted with some old friends." Mrs. Bainbridge leaned close to him. "You'll get used to your new name. Married women do it all the time."

Her declaration caught him off guard. She was correct, of course, but he had never considered the impact.

"I'll take the invitation into consideration. I must admit that I'm overwhelmed with the number of invitations I've received to dinners, country weekends, galas, and private dinners for two. Combine that with the letters from well-wishers, the borough representative, various people in Parliament, the Lord Mayor, and other barristers in the Inns of Court. I didn't think I would have to be concerned about my social calendar here. I thought I left all that behind in London."

"Ah, you have caught the eye of every mother in the *ton* with an eligible daughter." Barrington pounded him on the back.

Willbury nodded his agreement as he absentmindedly thumbed the ducal ring he now wore.

"Widows and courtesans as well. And I don't have time to show my face in London society," he interjected.

"I don't think they are looking at your face, my lord." Barrington tried not to laugh. "It's your pockets they are most interested in seeing intimately."

He stared at Barrington, his eyes glowing in amusement until he let out a hearty laugh.

"I am aware." Willbury worked to regain his composure. "It's one of the reasons I'm here in Sommer-by-the-Sea."

"One of the reasons? Are there others?" Barrington's voice held a smile.

"I've spent the last month in London going over Aunt Adelaide's estate. Uncle John passed last October. I was out of the country for the Crown. I returned in December and was hailed as the new Duke of Willbury. Without an entail, my uncle left The Willow to Aunt Adelaide.

"My aunt assured me she could manage the estate at least until I settled my affairs in London. It appears she allowed her accounts to be handled by someone under-skilled and overwhelmed. When I arrived for her funeral last month, I gathered the journals. They were not in good order. Rather than manage the issue from London, I've decided to take up residence at The Willow until I have things sorted out."

"I'm surprised your aunt employed someone who was not up to snuff. I thought she was very shrewd and perceptive when it came to managing her estate and affairs. More so than many a gentleman I've come to know."

"Honoria, you visited with the duchess often, how did she seem to you?"

"I saw her every week since His Grace's passing. We sat together in her bedroom to have a hot cup of cocoa. I was with her the evening before her accident. We went over the broadsheets. She commented on everyone mentioned. She was in good spirits, tired, but comfortable and content. I asked why she wore a priceless piece of jewelry to sleep. She told me the story of the brooch, and how she wore it every night on her nightrail. It was a marriage gift from His Grace, and she wore it every night since his passing. You might consider that eccentric, but as Reese mentioned, she was also shrewd and perceptive."

A dark cloud came over his former commanding officer's face. "No. It's not like her at all. You've secured—"

"The estate records, ledgers, and journals. Yes, under lock and key. So far, I've found nothing out of the ordinary. A few excessive bills, nothing more. But I've only started my investigation."

"I strongly suggest you speak to Judge Scofield." Barrington leaned forward and stared at him for a moment. "If you want a casual meeting, he'll be at the soiree tomorrow evening. He may be able to help you. Do you expect foul play?"

"Not exactly. My aunt insisted on continuing her charity work. She successfully took on many causes. We all told her she should curtail her activities for health reasons. But she wouldn't listen. She said with pride that if she listened to what people told her she never would have married her dashing duke and lived a life filled with happiness, mutual admiration, and companionship. Aunt Adelaide lived life as she wanted and, in the end, died content and happy. It is possible that it became too much for her although I wouldn't have thought so."

Barrington eyed Mrs. Bainbridge with a gleam of tenderness, then turned to his friend. "I know few women of her caliber. Her Grace was elegant, petite, intelligent, and generous. Her Grace's legacy is much greater than the Reinsford family fortune."

A gentle smile tipped the corners of Willbury's lips.

"A much greater legacy. And regarding that wicked sense of humor that you said she possessed. I dined every Tuesday at her table when she was in residence in London. We discussed the latest theater production, a book she read, or news of the day. It was a guarantee when all that information was chewed into nothingness that the discussion turned to the case in which I was involved. Aunt Adelaide told me what I needed to do, usually before dessert was served. I could set my timepiece by it."

They all chuckled. "She was a wonderful lady."

"But?" Barrington asked.

"Talking about my current case gave her license to talk about more personal issues. Her favorite question was when did I plan to marry and who will I choose. *When will you settle down Fraser? You're not going to be one of those doddering old codgers so set in your ways that no one will have you, are you?*'

'She repeated those exact words so often that one evening when I said it with her without missing a beat, she became flummoxed. I, on the other hand, had the audacity to chuckle. She rose from her chair and retired from the dining room. I drank my wine, giving her time to gather herself.

When I quit the room, her butler handed me my hat and coat and said good night. It appeared Aunt Adelaide had retired for the evening."

"Oh, dear. Not very gracious of her." Mrs. Bainbridge's hand covered her mouth.

Willbury turned to her with an exasperated expression.

"My feelings, exactly. In the morning, I sent her a bouquet of chrysanthemums, her favorite flower, with a card that said it would take me at least until I was a doddering old codger to find a woman like her. I would accept no one less."

"A lovely gesture." Mrs. Bainbridge removed her hand and graced him with a satisfied smile. "And she forgave you?"

"Her footman delivered an invitation to dessert that evening, to finish our meal. She still asked when I would marry every time we dined. Now, she has the final laugh. My aunt was well aware how much I loved her and The Willow. Her will states that I must be married within twelve months of the will's reading, or I forfeit inheriting the estate."

"Protect the line." Barrington pounded his walking stick on the floor for emphasis.

"Precisely. At the moment, I appear to be a tempting morsel for mothers of daughters who are hungry for a match. And not for my winning personality, mind you. Need I say more? That is only one of my obligations. I am much better suited to working through the scrambled situation in which I find her estate. I wasn't raised to be a duke."

"I'm glad to help you along with questions about the dukedom. As a second son, my father saw to it that I understood my responsibilities should Edward not be able to carry on."

He had no doubt Barrington could be counted on. Even as boys, he was dependable and the essence of loyalty and honor. Barrington proved him right when they served together.

"Many a duke is trained from the time they're toddlers and molded by the past. You are fortunate." Barrington was more serious than usual. "You have the ability to choose the type of duke you want to be."

Willbury raised his eyebrow at Barrington's statement. At that moment, he understood the awesome responsibility he'd inherited. In order to manage the dukedom, he had to understand the workings of the past, the needs of the present and, more importantly, the possibilities for the future.

"You're either a man who works for the betterment of his constituency or for his own personal gain. The rewards for the first type of man brings you much more than blunt. Consider that your first lesson."

Barrington and Mrs. Bainbridge stared at him for several minutes. His friend's statement didn't surprise him. It is how the man judged himself.

"Good morning."

The soft voice behind him, Anna's voice, had every nerve in his body and brain at attention. He turned and was rewarded with her smile. He stood and let out a breath as she drew closer.

She floated over to the small group with a package in her hand. What happened to the hoyden he remembered? Bronze curls, mostly hidden by her bonnet, framed her face. Her frame was slender, her hips slim. But it was her penetrating brown eyes that made him catch his breath. They were still full of mischief and good humor. Lovely and guileless as ever.

Anna drew up beside him. "What a pleasant surprise. I wasn't aware you returned to Sommer-by-the-Sea." She gave him a small curtsy and peeped at him under her brows. "Congratulations on the bestowal of your title, Your Grace."

"I'm still the same Fraser." They shared a smile. His was almost apologetic while hers was... mysterious.

A pang of guilt made beads of sweat form on his lip. Thankfully, his mustache absorbed the dampness. In the last five years, Anna had been in London several times during the social Season. He had been invited to the Ravencroft's London house several times but declined claiming pressing business. In retrospect, he should have made time for them. Visiting old friends after leaving the service was too painful without his brother by his side. Surely, they understood.

"Of course, you're Fraser, but now you're also a duke with all the pomp and circumstance that goes with the title. Enjoy it." Anna took a step back and eyed him up and down, then leaned closer. "It fits you well, Your—"

He put his finger to her lips before she voiced his appellation. The touch of her soft lips against his forefinger was not only scandalous but dangerous. Thank goodness they were sequestered in a small alcove with no one other than Barrington and Mrs. Bainbridge.

Her startled expression faded as fast as it rose. However, the heat that simple touch ignited burned with a lasting impact and sent beads of moisture rolling down his back.

Anna opened her mouth to speak but hesitated and remained deep in thought for several seconds. At last, she went on. "Is the title so offensive?"

Her soft voice and the movement of her moist lips mesmerized him. "No, not offensive."

"Ah, the fabric doesn't yet fit."

A small smile tipped the corners of his mouth as he nodded.

"It will. If anyone is a cut above and a leader of men, it is you, Fraser Castleton. The duchess, may her memory be a blessing, was fortunate to have a devoted, valiant man to assume the responsibility. You will be a brilliant 8th Duke of Willbury."

"Hear, hear." Barrington and Mrs. Bainbridge added their agreement.

"The new Duke of Willbury is residing at The Willow." Barrington swung around to face him, then glanced at Lady Anna. "Lady Anna, I'm hosting a small soiree tomorrow evening for some close friends. I would be honored if you would join us. Judge Scofield, Peter Simms, Simon Watts, and their wives will be joining Honoria and myself. You and Willbury would round out the table nicely."

"Lady Anna, should we humor him?" Willbury leaned toward her.

Anna got on her tippy toes and peered over his shoulder, then leaned close to him. "Perhaps. I don't think he will stop unless we do. Do you have any idea why he is so adamant?"

"I find myself being eyed by mothers—"

"Oh, say no more." She gave him a big smile. "Even more reason to attend Lord Reese's soiree. I am happy to accompany you and once again play your protector."

"Once again? Surely, you're not counting that time—"

"I am. And rightly so. You fell in the mud. Who was there to protect your back from Mrs. Cutler's rolling pin?"

The four began to laugh but quickly remembered where they were.

"Think of Lady Anna as your secret weapon against eager mothers." Barrington put his arm around his friend. "Have no fear, my friend. It's all part of being a duke."

"I must be on my way. Mrs. Bainbridge, thank you for tea. I had a lovely time. It was good to see you." Anna turned to leave.

"I'll see you home." Willbury extended his arm.

With a brilliant smile, Anna placed her hand on his arm. They said a quick farewell and took leave of the library.

"I am so sorry about your aunt's passing. She was a unique and wonderful woman." They walked along King's Way toward the north end of the village.

"That she was. It's difficult to go through the house and not feel her presence. I haven't gotten used to the estate being mine. Although having Kaiah is a big help. She nearly knocked me over when I arrived. The dog has no sense how big she is."

They walked on for a while.

"I never trained to be a duke." He remained quiet for a few minutes. "Men spend their lives learning their ducal responsibilities. I need a greater understanding before I assign responsibilities to others. And then there's meeting everyone. If I said yes to every invitation, I would get nothing done." He put his hand over hers. "Today, I took time for myself, and I'm glad I did."

They walked on enjoying the day and each other's company as they turned down the ash and clay drive to Raven Hall.

That was so like him. He always needed the details before he did anything. She supposed that's what made him a fine barrister. She gave him a sideways glance. He was still deep in thought. He would be a very fine duke. The duchess's beloved estate couldn't have been passed on to a better person.

The door opened as they came onto the porch. She turned to him.

"There is a way to solve your problem."

He shot her a quizzical glance.

"Invite everyone to a reception at The Willow. You'd meet them all at one time, along with those scheming mothers."

"It sounds painful." He comically cringed at the thought.

Anna's laugh made him smile. "You wouldn't want the reception at your London residence, would you?"

"Not at all." His quick response didn't surprise her. Holding the reception in London would increase the guest list.

"I thought not. As for the reception being painful." She put her hand on his chest and spoke softly. "Not nearly as painful as having to deal with those individual invitations."

His mouth twitched with amusement before he turned serious. "Where to begin?"

"I'll help you."

Her remark seemed to catch him off guard.

"I can't impose." A bit of panic colored his voice.

"Yes, you can. We can have a reception the Sunday after next. It would be reminiscent of the receptions your aunt hosted every Sunday. Your housekeeper is your best asset."

He stared at her, evaluating the plan, then laughed. The sound was deep, rich, and warm. "Very well. When should I tell Mrs. Barton to expect you?"

"Tomorrow, if you please." Helena Barton was an excellent housekeeper and took great care of the duchess. "Thank you for seeing me home."

"My pleasure." He touched the brim of his hat. "I'll collect you tomorrow evening at 7:30. You have me looking forward to dinner."

She tilted her head and gave him a soft, mischievous smile. "I'm looking forward to dinner, too."

Chapter Three

Anna hurried into the house. She couldn't get to the front window fast enough. She peeked out and kept Fraser in sight as he walked down the path. She still detected the essence of the young man she remembered, the confident way he carried himself, and the aura of command that fit him like a second skin.

She stepped away from the window but stole one final glance as he turned onto King's Way. It was good to have her friend back, and she was happy to help him.

Turning away from the window, she surveyed the room. Pale-green fabric and white painted trim covered the walls. Furniture upholstered with Jacobean floral print fabric with yellow and peach roses, snapdragons, and carnations was well positioned around the room. The colors were picked up in the drapery and carpet. The two floor-to-ceiling windows that flanked the fireplace faced the garden. Each color, each piece of furniture added to the creation of a bright and welcoming room.

This room is where she and her mother received morning calls and served tea, where the family gathered in the evenings to read, discuss the latest news and the day's events, and where she retreated after her two dismal Seasons. In a word, this was her sanctuary.

She sat at her desk, took out paper, and prepared her quill. She paused and stared out at the garden. It was hard to believe nearly ten years had passed since Willbury—she too had to get used to his new name—and Lucian went off to fight Napoleon. They wrote to each other for the first year, but mail from the Continent became scarce and finally stopped. Not long afterwards, they received news of Lucian's death.

She stroked her cheek with the quill. The last time they spent time together was when she gave him Kaiah. They were the closest of friends. Well, that was then. They are both different people now, but they'd always be friends.

"The morning mail." Mrs. Cutler placed the salver on her desk.

"It's been a long time since a new duke has established residence in the area. I told Fraser I would assist him in planning a reception, a come out of sorts. His arrival shouldn't go unnoticed." She put down her quill, picked up one of the messages, and opened it. "He doesn't like to be called His Grace. Willbury is fine, he says."

"Will he be hosting his coming out at his London home?"

She lowered the message and gave the woman her attention. The picture Mrs. Cutler painted of a man coming out as a debutante had Anna shaking her head.

"No, His Grace will be introduced to his guests at The Willow." For a moment, she thought Mrs. Cutler had an odd look about her. It must be her imagination. "People haven't been to the estate since the duchess took ill after Lord Willbury's passing. Everyone will want to see the country house and meet the new duke."

"You mean every mother with an eligible daughter will want to be there to make their claim on a very eligible, wealthy, and handsome man. For many, it will be their last event before they are all off to London for the Season. A family would relish starting the Season with the Duke of Willbury joining their family."

"That, too. He mentioned that he removed himself from London to get away from that circus. I do not blame him. I remember that all too well." No. She had never in her life felt so degraded, on show like a prize horse.

Two fruitless Seasons. Perhaps not totally fruitless. She did have several opportunities, but they weren't gentlemen with whom she wanted to spend the rest of her life or have children. She shuddered at the idea.

A part of her, deep down, questioned why she hadn't attracted someone more… more what? Her mother told her to accept one of the suitors. All the gentlemen who offered for her were well educated, not intimidated by her independence, titled, and moderately situated. None needed Ravencroft money. But there wasn't anything exciting about them, and more importantly, they equated an independent woman to a young man sowing his wild oats. Once married, the woman would of course conform to propriety. As if a woman's life stopped when she married. None of them offered for *her*. Plain and simple, they offered to relieve of her of her money.

Anna's fingers crushed the corner of the message in her hand. Her mother was more than willing to trot her out for another Season. Never. She would rather be a withered old maid than go through that humiliation again.

"When would he like to have his reception?"

She looked at Mrs. Cutler, surprised to see the housekeeper standing next to her.

"The Sunday after next, in the afternoon. The same time that Duchess used to have her receptions. Willbury needn't be too involved, nor does he need to be coached on what is expected. He only needs to be introduced to those attending. I think Mrs. Bainbridge could be his hostess." She glanced at the paper in her hand.

"That sounds like a fine plan. I understand there is reduced staff at The Willow."

Anna read the letter while she answered. "Find out who on our staff we can spare." Anna raised the sheet as she read silently. "I will be speaking to Mrs. Barton."

"Would you like a cup of tea?"

Anna read the document again. This must be a mistake. Richard wouldn't be sending his bills here. The tailor must have misunderstood.

The soft sound of cloth rustling by the door made her raise her head in time to see the housekeeper leave. Anna shoved the parchment into a folio. She'd handle this message at the appropriate time.

With an invisible shake, she wished she had said yes to that cup of tea, with a healthy splash of her father's whiskey.

Chapter Four

Francis Younge, an upright and just man, was an excellent representative of the people in his borough and a successful Member of Parliament. He'd held the prestigious position for twenty years.

Younge had been a welcome visitor at Raven Hall, coming often to speak to Anna's father, and from time to time, her parents hosted a reception in his honor. However, eight years ago something was said or done that put them at odds. Anna had no idea what caused the breach, but whatever happened resulted in the ceasing of all visits and communication between the two families. Others saw the Younge family move to the other side of the borough, close to the Scottish border, an explanation to fewer visits.

The letter from Francis Younge appeared two weeks ago. It took a minute or two for her to fully understand his request.

> 24 August 1814
> Dear Lady Marianna,
> I must step down from my position both from being a representative for the borough and the House of Commons. I am in poor health. My son, your cousin Richard, is set to take my place, and I am hoping for the good of our family that you will help him in any and every way that you can. Your skills as a hostess are well known. I think your help with a reception for the voters would see him well.
> I remain,
> Francis Younge

The lack of any gracious opening startled and bothered her. Francis never brought up their familial relationship in the past. He was her father's third cousin. That made Richard her… her fourth cousin. The upcoming election was six weeks away. It would begin the fifth of October and conclude on the sixth of November. The abrupt nature of the message and the fact that the request was made to her and not her father could be due to the family's estrangement. Is this plea a way to begin the healing process? A hasty decision would not do.

In the end, she decided helping with a reception was the least she could do to bring the families back together.

Richard presented himself at Raven Hall before she penned a reply. He was rough around the edges and needed instruction from the appropriate clothes to wear to the finer social skills.

As far as campaigning, his needs were limited. The borough was a small one. He could easily meet and speak to all the voters at a reception. His sponsor would provide the location. He needed her assistance with the invitations and menu. Together they planned to hold the event on the fourth of October, the day before the election began.

By the end of the afternoon, Richard proved that he took his campaign seriously. He was a likable sort, although at times he pressed his point too hard and took liberties when he should know better. She attributed his missteps to a young man eager to make his own mark in the world. He was capable of learning the social graces. Perhaps that is why his father had reached out to her.

Here it was two weeks later, and she still struggled to secure what she needed from him. He begged her forgiveness and said he would provide what she requested, but the next time she saw him he only had a portion of what she required. There were times she wished she had sent his father her regrets, but Richard would ask for her forgiveness, promise to do better, and besides, now it was too late.

"Anna." She turned as Richard entered the drawing room. Mr. Cutler hurried behind him.

"I'm sorry, my lady." It wasn't often that her butler was frazzled.

She glanced from Richard, who stood at the window looking out at the garden, to her butler.

"Quite all right, Mr. Cutler." She gave him a smile, hoping to quiet his nerves. "That will be all."

The butler squared his shoulders and exited with his dignity intact.

"You shouldn't barge into a room unannounced." She opened the folio and read the bill she received from the tailor.

Richard turned from the window and glared at her. "I do at home."

He sounded like a petulant child rather than someone her own age of twenty-four.

Anna put down the document, clasped her hands, and glared back at him. "Ah, but you don't barge into a room unannounced in a house that isn't yours."

A rush of pink surged up his neck, leaving his pale skin covered in spots. They coordinated nicely with his new vest. Although with his red hair, she wouldn't have chosen a yellow brocade.

His coat was tailored well enough to hide his sloped shoulders. His face was plain. His smile and bright disposition carried it along. However, she hadn't seen that side of him lately.

She didn't mean to embarrass him, but he had to learn the protocol of Society, especially if he planned to sit in Parliament and be taken seriously.

He lowered his head. "When will I learn?" He lifted his shoulders in a half shrug while an easy smile played at the corners of his mouth.

"I'm sure you will." Anna shook her head. "I am glad you're here. Do you have the names of the additional guests? We really must get the invitations out. More importantly, you haven't told me where the reception is to be held."

"You needn't worry. The election is simply a formality. I am unopposed."

"A formality? If you are unopposed, why not celebrate your victory after the election rather than have a reception now. Surely your sponsor has better things to do with his money."

"I agree, but he says we must have a reception. Let's not worry about him. I can't stay long. I'm on my way to Newcastle. I came for the carriage, but I was told it was not at my disposal."

"Carriage? What happened to your carriage?" The smooth flirtatious smile he flashed at her was an overused tactic, at least where she was concerned.

"It's being repaired. My driver took it into a ditch." He marched up to her with both his hands on his hips. "I just realized I gave you a list. Can't you use that to write out the invitations?"

She tried to disguise her annoyance even though it was getting more and more difficult. Opening the desk drawer, she took out the partial list he had given her and laid it on the desk.

"I need two important pieces of information. A complete list. All the invitations must go out at the same time and where the reception will be held."

"You have most of the names." He stood towering over her and took the list that was on the desk.

She stood, putting them on an equal footing.

"Yes, you told me it wasn't complete and asked me to wait."

"This is not difficult, Anna. Send invitations to those on the list." He tossed the paper back onto the desk.

Perhaps not a petulant child, but a man out of his element. If he acted this way over a reception, how would he perform in Parliament?

"And where am I to send your guests?" She stared at him like an angry schoolteacher, and he squirmed like a naughty boy. She took full advantage of his discomfort. "If you can't provide the information that is needed, perhaps you should tell your sponsor there will not be a reception."

That got his attention. The candidate went through a renaissance, an enlightenment.

"Tomorrow, you will give me three things: the rest of the guest list, the venue for your reception, and"—she pulled the item from today's mail from the folio and flashed it in front of him—"where to send your bills. They are not to be sent here."

He stepped closer to her.

A sinister veil flashed over his face before it lit with one of his dazzling smiles, although this one did not reach his eyes.

"You're correct, of course. I've had so much on my mind. Tomorrow, I'll have the remaining names for you as well as where the reception is to be held." He took a breath, ready to speak, but remained quiet.

Anna waited a few heartbeats.

"Were you going to say something?"

"Never mind about the carriage." He waved his hand dismissively. "It would slow me down anyway. Riding to Newcastle will be faster."

He started for the door and paused at the threshold. "Tomorrow, Anna. I'll have everything you need tomorrow." And he was gone.

She grabbed her shawl, wrapped it closely around herself, and stepped out onto the garden patio, mumbling under her breath. "Send out invitations without the destination."

The weather was cool but invigorating. Perhaps it could temper her annoyance.

For several sweet minutes, she didn't have to manage Richard. Today's outburst wasn't the first, but it was progressing. The nerve of him assuming he had access to her carriage. That and his attitude were enough to…

Patience. He has much to learn. Once the arrangements are made for the reception, there will be relief, and life will get back to normal.

Thank goodness, Willbury's reception would be easier.

Anna walked under the arbor. He looked the same as she remembered. No, better. The wool of his jacket stretched across his broad shoulders and fitted him quite nicely. The way he stood, his gestures, aided in creating an air of command that was uniquely his.

Coming out of the arbor, she circled back toward the drawing room door, thinking that the image suited him well as a barrister.

His boyish awkward features were refined, chiseled into a mature handsome man. His blue-green eyes remained expressive. His face was covered with a well-trimmed beard. For a moment, she wondered if it was a remnant of his days in the service. His once wild hair was now cut romantically long and mostly tamed. The only remnant of its unruliness was a lock of hair over his brow that every so often fell into his eyes. He used to comb it back into place with his fingers. That brought a smile to her lips.

She climbed the steps to the patio and entered the drawing room.

For a moment, she imagined him in his judicial wig with that lock of hair hanging down. A loud chuckle escaped her lips. She quickly put her hand over her mouth. Willbury in a wig? On second thought, she imagined he would be quite fetching.

Mrs. Cutler entered and placed a cup of hot tea on her writing desk. "Happy, are we?"

"I was thinking of Fraser Castleton, 8th Duke of Willbury. The title fits him. I tried to conjure up what he might look like in his white powdered wig and long black gown. I decided he must be fetching." She caught sight of the blank invitations and let out a heavy sigh. "Enough about His Grace. I'll write Richard's invitations, or at least fill in what I can."

"Regarding Willbury's reception."

Anna caught the *Do you really want to talk about Richard* look in Mrs. Cutler's eyes. Shaking her head, she clasped her hands on the desk.

"I told His Grace we would assist Mrs. Barton."

Mrs. Cutler tilted her head and nodded. "I used to help with the weekly reception whenever Mrs. Barton needed an extra pair of hands. It will be good to work with her again."

Chapter Five

The following morning, Anna and Mrs. Cutler sat in The Willow's drawing room with Mrs. Barton. She didn't look like anyone special at all until she smiled. Then, even her gray muslin gown with its high-cut neck and long sleeves brightened.

"It's been a long time since we have had tea together." Mrs. Barton passed a platter of confections. "Her Grace enjoyed your visits."

"As did I. It's difficult to think she is no longer here." Anna studied her choices and placed a madeleine on her plate. "I keep thinking or hoping she will walk through the door and ask you to 'fortify' her tea."

"Her Grace would step into the room carrying her teacup. 'Helena,' she'd say, 'Something is wrong with this tea. Is there something amiss in the kitchen?' *No,* I would tell her. Then give her a splash of the very watered-down brandy. Dr. Manning had forbidden her to drink spirits. She never questioned the quality of her fortifier. I never stopped providing it for her."

The three women laughed, remembering the duchess's spirit.

"Her Grace liked her tea, her jokes, and her ginger biscuits." Mrs. Barton passed the ginger confection to her guests. "I'm so glad you're visiting today. It gave me a reason to make a larger batch of biscuits. His Grace seems to eat them all."

"And here I thought he liked my apple tarts." Mrs. Cutler took a sip of tea.

"He does. The man is very evenhanded. He likes your tarts and my biscuits." Mrs. Barton turned to Anna. "When His Grace mentioned a Sunday reception, I took the liberty of gathering the information from the last one the duchess hosted. It's hard to believe that was a year ago when the late duke began to decline. Stopping Sunday receptions was a difficult decision for her. The staff is happy to prepare The Willow for one again. I've made a copy of the last guest list for you."

Anna took the list and perused the names.

"Some people on that list have moved away and can be removed, and there may be others His Grace wants to add." Mrs. Barton nodded at the document as she poured tea. "I thought we would work on the list and give it to His Grace for the final review. In the meantime, the staff has been concentrating on an inventory of The Willow and Rein Hall, the London house. With His Grace taking over the estate and all, an accounting must be done."

"Inventory?" Mrs. Cutler asked. "You don't expect any–"

"Not at all," the housekeeper interrupted. "Some things are not where they belong. We are sure they have only misplaced a silver teapot, candlesticks given to them by the Queen, the late duke's sword, and several pieces of Her Grace's jewelry."

Helena Barton had worked at The Willow for over two decades. She had been a house maid and worked her way to become the housekeeper. Her position was well deserved. Anna noted a change in her tone, and it struck her. The woman was angry.

"Perhaps we've come at an inopportune time. I'm sure if you're in the midst of a major inventory you are needed elsewhere." Anna began to gather her things.

"Forgive me, Lady Anna. Mr. Barton and I have completed the inventory of the estate house and all its contents as His Grace requested. Mr. Barton will go over it with His Grace later today along with the inventory of the London House. There is no reason why we shouldn't move ahead with our planning." Mrs. Barton handed Anna a folio and pencil. "Here is the information I mentioned earlier."

Anna leafed through the pages for a cursory look. In addition to the guest list that Mrs. Barton had already handed her, she found an attendance record that went back five years, as well as a menu with comments noting how much of each item was consumed. The report was thorough and made repeating the event easy.

"The staff is proficient at putting this menu and event together. I thought with a week's notice it would be best to keep to the duchess's Autumn reception. The staff is familiar with the menu and house décor, although I would like to make this reception leave its own unique mark for His Grace. Would you consider assisting with the décor?"

"This is a relief." Anna read the menu. "Most of the planning is right here: the food, placement on the table, dishes to use. I have some ideas on how to make this event uniquely Willbury's."

"Thank you. You may want to add one or two items His Grace seems to enjoy." Mrs. Barton gave Mrs. Cutler a mischievous look. "He mentioned your apple tarts, Martha."

"You needn't say another word. I'll bring several dozen. Is additional staff needed?"

"The kitchen is well staffed. An additional two footmen would be helpful."

"You are right, Mrs. Barton. This menu will do nicely." Anna made several notations and handed the materials to Mrs. Cutler to review.

"The cider punch is one of my favorites. No one makes it like you. I look forward to it every fall. I remember Mama telling me when I was young to leave some for the other guests."

"We have two days to send out the invitations. There are many on this guest list I know must be invited. I can start writing out the invitations while you go over the list with His Grace. I can have all these completed by this evening. Mrs. Bainbridge will be hosting the event with His Grace. I'm to be a deterrent rather than a hostess."

Mrs. Barton raised an eyebrow at Mrs. Cutler.

"His Grace has been bombarded by mothers with eligible daughters of late. I am with him to protect him from their onslaught. We'll see if this strategy works."

"Her Grace took pride in choosing the flowers and décor for all her receptions. Come with me to the conservatory. We have some choices."

The women followed Mrs. Barton.

The driver handed down Anna and Mrs. Cutler from the carriage in front of Raven Hall.

"The Willow's salon is as I remember it. I was afraid the room would look tired and in need of some tender loving care, but Mrs. Barton and the staff have maintained it beautifully."

Anna, carrying the bouquet of flowers Mrs. Barton had given her, walked up to the front door with Mrs. Cutler.

"Good afternoon, Mr. Cutler."

He nodded at them.

"Let me take those, my lady, and get them into a vase. They'll look lovely on the salon table." Mrs. Cutler stood ready to take the flowers.

Anna took a whiff of the bouquet. The rich reds, deep oranges, and buttery yellows captured the warmth and beauty of the autumn season. "Come get me a little after six." She handed the bouquet to Mrs. Cutler and turned to her butler.

Mrs. Cutler nodded and went down the service hall.

"Did my cousin leave anything for me?" Anna looked at the butler and knew the answer by the look of annoyance on his face. A flash of frustration dampened her mood.

"Mr. Younge hasn't been here today, my lady." The butler was on his way to the servant's hall as Anna entered the drawing room.

She took the bundle of stationary with the duke's crest out of her reticule and put it on her desk. Without Richard's information, she had time to work on Fraser's.

Anna busily laid out the blank card with the Duke of Willbury seal, envelopes, quills, ink, and the guest list.

Fraser Castleton, 8th Duke of Willbury
Respectfully requests the company of
The Reverend W. Hendrickson
to a Sunday Reception at The Willow on the 18th day of September 1814
between 1 and 4 o'clock in the afternoon.

The task went quickly. Sixty-five invitations were completed and stacked on Anna's desk. As she dipped her quill into the ink to start the next invitation, a loud voice in the hall caught her attention.

"No need, Cutler. I know the way."

"May I?" was all he asked as he stood at the door.

"Good afternoon, Richard. Do come in." Small gains should be rewarded.

He strutted in front of her carrying a folio, looking like Beau Brummell himself. He posed and waited for her to comment.

She laid her hand on the folio of bills, his bills, that she kept on her desk and remained quiet.

The flash of lavender at the door drew her attention. "I beg your pardon, Lady Anna. You asked to be reminded at six o'clock." Mrs. Cutler entered the room and came up next to her.

Richard glared at the lavender gown cascading over her arm, then at Anna.

Over the years, Mrs. Cutler honed her dismissive stare intended to unnerve people. She was particularly successful with Richard. The woman didn't need to say a word to make Richard uncomfortable.

He moved closer, planting himself next to Anna, forcing her to look straight up at him.

Richard never stayed long in Mrs. Cutler's company. Today, he all but claimed his territory. Perhaps his expensive new clothes gave him bravado.

He craned his neck to see what she worked on.

She shot him an angry glance while she turned over the invitation, annoyed at his behavior and galled he forced her to conceal what she was doing in her own home.

"Thank you, Mrs. Cutler. If you wait a moment, I'll need your help upstairs."

Anna observed his state of mind change from disorientation to confusion, and finally, his eyes glowed in a scalding fury.

"You're not going anywhere." His whispered words were clearly a challenge.

She stared at him, making an effort to control her building anger.

"This visit is over." Anna's voice was calm and sweet.

Richard didn't move.

"I am certain Mr. Cutler can help you find the door." His attitude may have surprised her, but she would not tolerate his insolence, family or not.

He ignored her warning.

"These aren't my invitations." He raised his arm ready to sweep the stack of cards onto the carpet.

Anna sprang from her seat, grabbed his wrist, and squeezed until she was satisfied that he understood her intention. Mrs. Cutler hurried out the door.

"You said my invitations had to be delivered tomorrow. You haven't finished them. You can't go anywhere."

Anna dropped his hand.

"You must take care of my event." He handed her the folio he carried. "I've brought the guest list."

Anna opened the folio and leafed through the various sheets of paper.

"There is no need for you to review what's there. I scrutinized the names carefully. These are the people you're to invite. I'm sure you can get these all delivered by tonight." He moved close to her.

She put the papers back into the folio and placed it on the desk.

"First, Richard, I will remind you to whom you are speaking. You do not tell me what to do. Ever. Second, you still haven't told me where the reception is being held. Third, no, the invitations will not be going out tonight. And finally, to whom do I send the bills?" She pulled documents out of her folio and gave him a handful.

"I've made changes to the reception plans." He put the bills on her desk and paced in front of her massaging his wrist.

"What sort of changes?" He wasn't looking at her. *What has he gotten himself into now?*

He stopped pacing and glared at her. "The hall that I planned for the reception is no longer available."

"I thought your sponsor owned several halls from which you could choose."

"I took one look at the places and my heart sank. He is sponsoring several campaigns. He provided a hall to each of us. The one for me is all wrong. He wanted me to have the reception in a barn. A barn."

"What's wrong with a barn? All the voters in the borough are farmers. They would be comfortable in a barn." Mrs. Cutler was right. This was going to be a disaster. "When did you know where your sponsor wanted your reception?"

"I found out three maybe four days ago. And before you ask, I didn't say anything yesterday because I was trying to find another location." He started pacing again.

"You should have told me. Perhaps you can speak to the Millers. They have a reception room at the library." She wanted to scream at him. Instead, she contained her anger.

"This isn't the only issue I'm working on. There are other important things that need my attention." He took a breath to calm himself and struck a flirtatious pose, smile and all. "And is there really an issue? I can have the reception here."

His words were playful, but his meaning was sincere.

Anna's patience was stretched thin, to the snapping point.

"Here? No. You. Will. Not." Her voice was cold, exacting, each word spaced out evenly.

He had to know he had gone too far. From the panic in his eyes, she sensed desperation.

"Our families have been estranged for far too long. My mother mourns the loss of her dear cousin and good friend. Father may not say it, but he, too, is upset. Last year, when I discussed filling my father's seat, I saw an opportunity to heal our family's wound. And so did my father. I told them you were helping me. I have never seen him and my mother so pleased. At the end of the day, it is all about family."

The family was important to her, too. Was he simply overzealous and in need of more instruction and discipline? Her resolve weakened, but not to the point where she would surrender Raven Hall. The guest list had serious flaws. But there may be a way to handle it. Before she took action, she needed to better understand his goal. Did he want to attract voters or make the statement that he was his own man and not an extension of his father? It might work.

"I will admit, the Ravencroft name will go far in attracting the right people. It's the reason why I enlarged the guest list." He came over to her and took her hand. "We're so close. The election begins in two weeks."

"Richard, this was to be a small event at a local hall for the fifteen voters and several special guests from the district. There are nearly eighty people on your list. You have people here who will not mix well. What does your sponsor say about this?"

He dropped her hand and returned to his pacing.

"I met with Mr. Spivey and several other candidates he is sponsoring. They are in the larger boroughs, and they are also planning receptions."

Her stomach sank. Now she understood. Richard was the sort that didn't like being out done. Was that the real reason behind this event?

"I invited the current members of Parliament in the county along with several businessmen and some industrialists. Perhaps even a lord or two." He took a deep breath, turned, and faced her. "I told them the reception would be here."

She stepped back in shock.

"I may have gotten carried away," he quickly added, "but you'll take care of things. You know what to do." He pulled out his pocket watch. "I have a meeting I must attend. I'm sure with you handling all the details that everything will turn out fine."

He headed for the door. Mr. Cutler entered, followed by Mrs. Cutler.

"Let me understand."

He stopped midstep.

"You invited eighty people to my house. My house, not yours, and told them the reception was here without asking me." She kept her voice low and controlled.

For a brief moment, a shadow of hardened determination passed over his innocent expression. "Between the benefit to the family and Father's assurance, promises have been made making it necessary to have the reception here. I spoke with Mr. Spivey and tried to reason with him."

"You and Mr. Spivey have a great deal of audacity, but no authority to promise my home."

"Anna, we work well together. Perhaps it was fate that your two Seasons in London were fruitless. Without a commitment, you are free to focus on me and put your own things aside." He motioned to the invitations on her desk. "Afterward, together, I will take care of you, and you will help me do wonderful things for the borough."

Anna blinked, her mouth gaping open, her chest heaving.

Richard shot a look between Anna, the butler, and Mrs. Cutler.

"I know this is sudden, but I know you won't let your family, my father, or me down. I should think with a more impressive guest list that we should have more than tea and biscuits, a light supper perhaps."

He had the good sense to say nothing more and quickly leave the room. Mr. Cutler followed him out.

She stared at the door.

"Light supper? And who is paying for his light supper? Surely not you."

"You never did like Richard." Anna still stared after him.

"And for an excellent reason. That man is getting bolder. I wouldn't be surprised if he expected a full course meal and entertainment. And all for a rotten borough of fifteen people and ten cows. Up until now, his remarks have been carefully worded and covered with platitudes. How dare he mention your London Seasons. You did understand his weakly veiled insinuation?"

Afterward, together, I will take care of you, and you will help me do wonderful things for the borough.

"Yes, with your money. I know what you're thinking. Are you supposed to be grateful to him?"

Her housekeeper was right. But she had given her word and didn't want to shatter the peace between the families.

"He talks about being a member of Parliament and what he will do. He is excited and enthusiastic. No harm in that. He got carried away today, that's all."

"He didn't ask, mind you. He told you." Mrs. Cutler paused. "Do you hear yourself? Did you understand what he said? Are you willing to accept his proposal? The gentlemen you refused were one hundred times better than him, and you said no to all of them. All. Of. Them."

"He asked no such thing. He is part of my family and wants to impress his constituency and sponsor. That's not important now. We both know the best way for him to accomplish that is at a social evening." Anna took a sip of tea. "I'll see if the library is available and tell him the reception is there."

"The people he is inviting all know who and what Richard Younge is." Adamant, Mrs. Cutler leaned closer to Anna. "He wasn't nice as a boy, never taking responsibility for his actions, and he isn't nice as a man."

"Are you still angry about him taking the tarts?" Anna chuckled, trying to bring down the tone of the discussion.

"He didn't take one tart or even two. He took all of them. He didn't eat them or even give them to his friends, if he even had any. He dumped all the tarts into the pig pen and lied when Mr. Cutler caught him. He claimed he knew nothing about it. He hasn't changed. He simply hides his lies better. Cousin Richard is in for a sad awakening, and in the end, he will blame everyone else for his failures." The housekeeper's voice softened, "Including you."

Anna didn't want to admit it, but the woman was right. Hadn't he just blamed her for the invitations not being ready when it was his responsibility to give her the information she needed? Anna took out a piece of paper and wrote a note.

"Please ask Mr. Cutler to have this note delivered to the Duke of Willbury."

"You're not going?" Mrs. Cutler's face paled.

"Of course, I'm going. I want to go over this list before I leave. I'll meet Willbury at Lord Reese's."

Chapter Six

"Your Grace, will you be returning to London for the Season?"

Willbury sat across from Mrs. Scofield, the judge's wife. She monopolized him as soon as he walked in. She grabbed onto him like Kaiah with her bone, unwilling to relinquish it. She kept the conversation in play. He listened, however, if anyone asked what she said, he would be at a loss for words.

His back was to the window. It was not by any accident where he positioned himself. He had a clear view over Mrs. Scofield's right shoulder of the hall door. With this view, he could see everyone who entered the room. He wasn't certain if he was eager to see Anna for her company or to avoid listening to women tell him they, and only they, had the perfect match for him.

"At the moment, I'm planning to stay in Sommer-by-the-Sea." The judge's two daughters were married. He wondered who Mrs. Scofield wanted to promote to be his duchess. He smiled and nodded every so often as she went on about the daughter of a friend's sister who he must meet.

"Violet, are you bending His Grace's ear about Sonia's niece?" The judge took a seat next to his wife and turned to him. "I thought she had her heart set on a certain young baron."

"There is nothing definite. And a baron? Why, Lord Willbury is a duke." Mrs. Scofield gave him a coy smile, as if that would excuse her thinking of his title and not him, the man.

"Mrs. Scofield. I am honored that you would consider me for your friend's niece." Willbury tried to stifle his smile. "But far be it for me to come between true love."

The woman snapped open her fan and busied herself cooling down her annoyance and the rush of heat that turned her neck various shades of dark pink.

"Now, my dear." The judge put a gentle hand on his wife's shoulder. "If you'll excuse us, I have matters to discuss with His Grace."

The woman glared at her husband and answered with a small nod.

Willbury stood, excused himself, and gladly followed the judge to the other side of the room.

"Please forgive my wife. She is forever trying to play matchmaker. I thought she had her fill with our daughters. They did marry well but not because of anything she did. My daughters had a clear vision of what they wanted and when they found him, well, my wife and I are more than pleased with the results."

"No apology needed. I find there are two conversations people initiate with me. They are either looking for free legal advice or know someone I should marry." They came up next to Barrington.

"I see the judge rescued you." Barrington handed him a drink.

Willbury accepted the glass. He did look forward to the evening with Anna, but when her note arrived in the late afternoon, he feared she wanted to beg off. He was relieved, reading she would be delayed and would meet him here. Now, he took a sip of whiskey to hide his smile. He looked forward to having her by his side to deter the "Mrs. Scofields" that knew "just the young woman for him."

"We wanted to speak to you in confidence. Scofield and I were discussing the upcoming election. There seems to be gentlemen running for Parliament in several of the rotten boroughs."

"There are more rotten boroughs than I realized." Willbury sipped his drink. "It really is an indication of the current state of affairs. In some boroughs, a large portion of the population has moved away from the farms and into the cities, depopulating the district yet it retains its original representation."

"The phenomenon started about 1750 and has steadily grown," the judge added. "Now, sixty-five years later, the population in London has doubled at the expense of the countryside. It's the same here in Sommer-by-the-Sea. I see it in my courtroom. With expansion comes growing pains."

"That's a very tactful description. By growing pains, you mean abuses that impact the exploited, without the opportunity to be treated fairly. You and I both see it in the courts and, to a greater extent, lingering on our streets." Willbury spoke with certainty based on his experience with the disputes on his London desk. "Your rulings here proceed you. I have cited your judgements. You have my undying respect." Willbury lifted his drink and took a sip in a salute.

"The abuses don't stop with the manufacturer and the task masters who are employed to squeeze every minute out of the men, women, and children." Barrington took a fortifying sip of the whiskey. "Now they look to expand into politics. The industrialists are clever. They, or at least one man in particular, has decided to sponsor several young inexperienced candidates"—Barrington turned to the judge—"and have them to do his bidding with the intent of his protégés creating laws in his favor."

"Yes. The man is crafty. He doesn't want to control one borough. He wants to control several, like a puppet master." Scofield's voice was cold and as clear as ice. "He grooms these young candidates by providing them with money, tells them where to live, and who to marry. I don't like the idea of this strong outside source manipulating the House of Commons. At the moment, it appears every one of the rotten borough candidates supports the Tories in Parliament, even though the people they represent are suffering and would be better served by the policies of the other party."

"I'm well aware of the political differences between the Tories and the Whigs." It was an old rant that Willbury professed. "The Tories see themselves as righteous defenders of the country, the Church of England, and a strong ruling monarch. They are determined to keep things as they are, with their vision of imperialism and establishing Britain as the greatest world power.

"World power. What they mean is their own power. And at what cost? They plot and plan to fuel the war effort because there is money, a great deal of money, to be made by lending money to the English government, who is willing to pay high interest rates. While the Tories line their pockets, it's at the expense of the farmers, tradesmen, and day workers through meager salaries that aren't enough to house and feed their families."

"The veterans who stayed close to me, you included," added Barrington, "understand the war cost more than money. It's the cost of lives lost and families ruined."

"My brother Edward mentioned the Home Office is determined to shake loose the name of the industrial master mind. He's gone undetected long enough. It's time we put a name to this person. Peter and I spoke with Edward last week and gave him some information about a man we believe fits the modus operandi. Edward is taking the lead and is making inquiries. We should be receiving an answer soon."

"Is it possible a foreign influence is involved?" The very idea turned Willbury cold as he asked the question. Nothing would please the Little Emperor more than disrupting the English Parliament. He was thankful the man was safe on Elba Island. Barrington and Scofield had it right. An industrialist wanted to line his pockets.

"If you'll excuse me." Before he and Scofield said anything, Barrington was halfway across the room.

Willbury glimpsed where Barrington headed. It led to Mrs. Bainbridge. He smiled at seeing a softer side to one of the strongest, fear-provoking military leaders he knew. Looking at him now, it was difficult to remember that no one had expected Barrington to survive his war injuries.

Barrington's parents had summoned Dr. Manning to London to care for their second son, Reese. There had been no question that the doctor was a medical magician. But even the great Manning had thought Barrington was mortally wounded. His father stepped down from his ducal duties as the Duke of Northwood, asking Edward to take over the bulk of the responsibilities, in order to care for Reese.

Everyone rejoiced when the prognosis changed. It was the quality of life he would have that was the next concern. Barrington's parents summoned the men who meant the most to Reese, the ones who he'd led into war. Each would give their life for him.

More than medicine, Barrington's will to overcome his injury, along with the determination of his men to aid in his recuperation, was what brought him through that hell. No one thought he would ever be able to stand unsupported, much less walk. Thank the Lord, he proved everyone wrong.

"I've turned it over in my mind more times than I want to admit. I'm certain we're looking for a politician." Scofield pulled his attention away from Barrington and focused on Willbury. "An industrialist with his own agenda. He may be foreign, but I don't think so."

"What makes you say that?" Willbury had Scofield's undivided attention.

"There have been rumblings that this man cultivates and grooms the men. He wants a solid, upright looking person he can manipulate. The men he backs meet his needs. If you think my wife's matchmaking is bold and direct, then she's met her match. I've been told this sponsor chooses the wives of his protégés, making sure the women are wealthy. After they marry, he makes demands and begins to drain the women and their families through their husbands."

The hair on the back of his neck stood up at attention, but not because of anything the judge said. He shot a look at the entrance. He sensed that Anna was near and would walk through the doorway any moment. He wasn't disappointed.

♥ ♥ ♥

Five guests gathered near the hearth in soft conversation. Willbury and the judge were across from her. Barrington and Mrs. Bainbridge stood half hidden near the door to the garden. Anna made her way to her host.

"Good evening, Lord Reese."

"Lady Anna. I'm glad you were able to join us."

"Thank you for the invitation." She always thought Lord Reese a gallant man, courageous, honorable, dashing, and attentive. From the twinkle in the depths of his eyes, this evening he was attentive to Mrs. Bainbridge.

"Reese." Mrs. Bainbridge leaned close to Lord Reese.

The intimate use of Barrington's given name was not lost on Anna. She knew little about their relationship although, for years, she and several other graduates of Mrs. Bainbridge's Sommer-by-the-Sea Female Seminary speculated and made up their own story as young girls are wont to do.

"It seems the judge would like to speak to you." She nodded in the judge's direction.

Lord Reese followed her gaze, then turned to Mrs. Bainbridge. "I find the hardest part of hosting a dinner party is not being able to spend time with you."

Lord Reese's eyes brimmed with tenderness. Feeling a bit intrusive, Anna lowered her eyes, intent on brushing away an imaginary wrinkle in her gown.

"Reese, you are embarrassing Lady Anna."

The amused look vanished from Lord Reese's eyes. "Forgive me if I—"

"Oh no." Anna flashed a wide-eyed innocent gaze that transformed into a sincere, warm one. "Your secret is safe with me."

"You are kind." He took a breath, the concern fading from his face. "Alas, I must play the gracious host and see why I am being summoned. Stand ready. I may call for reinforcements."

"I am always ready to come to your aid, and you can be sure I'll bring the troops." Mrs. Bainbridge's soft laugh had Anna smiling as Lord Reese made his way to the judge and Willbury.

"Nothing drives the judge more than politics. Whenever he and Barrington are together, the borough's state of affairs is the primary topic of discussion. With Willbury's arrival in the village, he has a new audience who will listen." Mrs. Bainbridge turned to Anna. "You arrived at the right time. Violet Scofield cornered Willbury."

"Both Scofield girls are married." Anna noted the small group by the hearth where Violet Scofield held her own court of sorts. "You and I went to their weddings."

"You're quite correct. She bent his ear about her friend's niece."

Anna swallowed the flash of anger, squelching it before it ignited. Mrs. Bainbridge's mouth moved, but Anna heard only muffled sounds in her head. She took a cup of punch from a passing footman and sipped.

Her reaction was uncalled for. He was his own man and a very desirable one. There was more to him than his title and his wealth. She peered at him again. The thought of rekindling their friendship comforted her, but perhaps she was being naïve. The fond memories she had of the past were just that, the past. They cannot be brought back, only warmly remembered.

"…the girl hasn't been presented to Her Majesty and won't be for another two years."

"Two years? Why, that would make her fourteen." Anna gaped at Willbury. He smiled and dipped his head ever so slightly before he returned his attention to Lord Reese and the judge.

"Precisely. He is more than twice her age. Violet was disappointed when he told her he planned to remain in Sommer-by-the-Sea this Season."

A footman slid open the oversized pocket doors, revealing the dining room.

"Dinner is served."

Willbury and Lord Reese approached them. Willbury gave Anna his arm while Lord Reese led Mrs. Bainbridge away.

They walked past the judge and Mrs. Scofield, who took their place behind them.

"Jedidiah, those two make a lovely couple. You should have told me Willbury already had his eyes on someone. And Lady Anna. Yes, they do make a lovely couple. Well, it's Sonia's niece's loss."

Anna stopped. Willbury pulled her along without missing a step.

He bent close to her. "I am indebted to you. You haven't been here more than ten minutes, and you've already saved me."

"Mrs. Bainbridge mentioned as much. My circumstances are similar. You have no idea what the Mrs. Scofields of the *ton* feel compelled to share with me. They are appalled that I've had the poor taste to decline the attention of potential suitors. It makes them all the more eager to 'find the right gentleman' for me. Like your title, the Ravencroft legacy attracts... There's no need to tell you. You are quite aware that we are both in similar situations."

"You're correct. Perhaps we should work together. Of course, that would necessitate that we see each other every day and exchange strategies." They crossed the room toward the dining room. "I would give anything not to be the center of attention. No one cared who or what I did when I was simply a barrister."

"There was a time... I'm almost embarrassed to tell you."

He leaned down and spoke so only she could hear. "You must know your secrets are safe with me. Now that you've piqued my interest, you must tell me."

"That at one time I thought about wearing a token of some sort and letting people think someone had offered for me just to stop their infernal questions and interference."

They entered the dining room.

"I don't think that's so terrible." They browsed the table looking for their place card. "Look at Violet Scofield. She has it in her mind that we are interested in each other and is looking elsewhere for a match for Sonia's niece. There can't be any rumors of being after each other's fortunes. We've known each other almost all our lives, and we get along well."

She stopped and stared at him. He tugged her along.

"You're serious, aren't you?" The thought was intriguing. "No, it's impossible."

"Here we are. Conveniently next to each other." Willbury pulled out her chair. "I don't think it's impossible. A bit reckless, but nothing more. What obstacles could there be?"

He bent close as he moved her chair.

"We will be courting, not engaged. That will leave both of us able to discontinue the arrangement without consequences. Isn't that the purpose of courting? To see if we suit?"

She was more astonished that he was serious about this arrangement and not his usual teasing self.

He took his seat. "This will only work if everyone believes us." He leaned over to Mrs. Bainbridge next to him and said something she didn't hear.

Anna remained quiet. His idea was preposterous. It would require spending a great deal of time together. She gave him a sideways glance. Yes, she'd been thinking about him since yesterday, but this? And yes, they'd spent a lot of time together when they were younger, and she did miss her close friend.

He came away from Mrs. Bainbridge, chuckled, and returned his attention to her.

"I could always tell when you were conjuring up something. You are giving my proposition thought, aren't you?"

Anna dipped her head with all intentions of putting an end to his teasing. She schooled her face, presenting a stern haughty glare. She raised her chin and gazed into his eyes. The corner of his mouth twitched into his cheek, creating a mischievous mien.

His gentle laughter rippled through the air. His roguish eyes and lips released something inside her. She recognized his silent challenge. He thought he would accomplish what she could not.

"I can find you the right woman, eliminating the pressure those doting mothers present." She took her serviette and opened it onto his lap with a flourish. She worked hard to keep from grinning at calling his bluff.

"Meanwhile, I can get reacquainted with you, the *new* you. I wouldn't want to misrepresent you to any of my friends. Come to think of it…" She tapped her finger against her lips. "I can think of one or two ladies you would find acceptable."

"Yes. We've both changed over the last few years. I would like to get reacquainted. Without any commitment." He graced her with a devastating smile; the one that made her toes curl.

"I'd like not to be viewed as a prize racehorse with a winning purse." He nodded to the waiter who poured his wine.

She began to see how this arrangement would work well.

"And I will gladly be your standard bearer, an older brother of sorts. I pledge that I will get reacquainted with you and find you the perfect gentleman." He lifted his wine glass, nodded, and took a sip.

Willbury was the same playful boy she'd grown up with, although there were moments when she detected a sadness. She supposed that was to be expected.

"Will you join me at the tearoom tomorrow, or would you prefer to go riding?" He nodded to the footman who ladled soup into his bowl.

"Tomorrow?" She gave the footman room to serve her and observed Willbury as he elegantly took a spoonful. He was quite serious.

"Of course. There is no time to waste. The ladies, and the gentlemen, will be off to London for the Season soon. We want to have the pick of the crop. Do you think Mrs. Bainbridge would like to join us for tea?"

She turned to him, a spoon in her hand and her mouth agape. "A chaperone? You are serious."

"Recklessly determined. While you and I may be playing at courting, we still need to maintain propriety. I will not risk damaging your reputation. That would make finding you the right gentleman more difficult." He paused and gazed at nothing in particular. "Or it could make you more desirable."

She shook her head and dipped her spoon into the bowl, enjoying the gentle sparring as much as he did.

"When we find each other their perfect match, we can congratulate each other and remain ardent friends. Do you agree with our plan?"

She chewed her bottom lip and still found it difficult to believe he wanted to move forward.

Willbury smiled one of those smiles that lit his face. Her toes were already curled. This one melted her insides. She put down the spoon before she splashed soup on her gown.

"Yes, Your Grace."

"Oh, that will never do." His voice was velvet-edged as he put his hand over hers.

Her eyes widened. He had no idea how sensuous his voice sounded or his touch felt.

"What will never do?"

She didn't move her hand.

"Under the circumstances, you should call me Fraser, Anna." His voice was soft and warm. "Tell me again, you agree with the plan."

Anna studied his face for the joy of it. Her hand tingled beneath his. Surely, he could hear her heart banging against her chest. Was this how the successful girls felt after their Season? She took a deep breath and smiled at him, telling him how she felt without saying a word.

"Yes, Fraser. I agree with your plan, and I think asking Mrs. Bainbridge to join us for tea tomorrow is an excellent idea."

The man's smile brightened if that was at all possible. He turned toward his right.

"Mrs. Bainbridge, would you like to join Lady Anna and me for tea tomorrow afternoon at the Rostov Tearoom?"

The headmistress leaned forward. She scrutinized Anna, then Willbury. Anna nodded to the headmistress who, with great difficulty, tried not to smile.

"Your Grace, I would be honored to join you and Lady Anna tomorrow at tea."

Chapter Seven

Willbury rode down King's Way with its sentinel of trees dressed in their autumn foliage. The breeze tugged the red and gold leaves from their branches, releasing them to fly in a choreographed dance orchestrated by the wind. Willbury took a deep breath and enjoyed the woodland scent tinged with a hint of an ocean breeze as he drove on.

The carriage passed the other grand estates, turned up the drive to Raven Hall, and pulled up to the door. Willbury stepped down, carrying a bouquet of yellow and peach roses interspersed with white sweet william and sprays of lavender. He straightened his shoulders. Driven all morning by excited anticipation, he hurried to the porch and stepped up to the door. The manor door opened before he lifted the knocker.

"Good afternoon, Your Grace."

"Mr. Cutler." Willbury chuckled to himself as he removed his hat. The man had not changed. His thinning hair and receding hairline had not moved. His stern expression had not improved. When he was younger, he was certain the man practiced keeping a straight face. There was comfort in the fact that the butler was never out of character.

"I half expected you to address me as Master Fraser."

"Lady Anna and Mrs. Bainbridge are waiting for you in the drawing room." They solemnly moved down the hall. He shouldn't be surprised. It was the same stony Cutler he remembered.

He followed the butler. The man put his hand on the doorknob, then turned to him.

"You wear your title well, Your Grace."

Willbury took a surprised second glance. The man was smiling. Well, not with his lips, but with his eyes.

"It is my pleasure to welcome you once again to Raven Hall."

Cutler opened the door before Willbury had time to respond. He followed the man into the room.

"His Grace, the Duke of Willbury."

"Good morning, ladies." He stepped toward Anna and handed her the bouquet. "For you, Anna."

Her face colored nicely. There was honesty in blushing, a visual clue of her real emotion. Lovely. That's what she was.

"Thank you." She breathed in the bouquet's fragrance. "They are beautiful, Fraser."

"I'll see to them, my lady." Mr. Cutler took the flowers from her and left the room.

"Shall we, Your Grace?" Mrs. Bainbridge moved toward the door.

He pulled his gaze away from Anna and gawked at the headmistress. He had forgotten she was there.

"Of course." He held out his hand and gestured toward the door. "After you, Anna."

They filed out of the house to his waiting carriage.

Today, he wouldn't think about politics or his new estate. He sat back and relished the company and friendship of his companions. He sat across from the ladies who were in a deep conversation. The conversation between the two women was more than words. They communicated with their eyes, their movements, and even their silence.

Every so often Anna glanced at him, and he marveled at the way her excitement added a shine to her eyes and a polish to her cheek.

"Don't you agree, Your Grace?"

Willbury blinked at Mrs. Bainbridge, then shot Anna a look. Both women stared at him waiting for his response. He could feel his cheeks heat under his beard. How should he respond? Honestly.

"Half a truth is often a great lie, according to Benjamin Franklin. So, the whole truth… ladies, forgive me. I was enjoying the ride and your company."

"You didn't hear the question." Mrs. Bainbridge's voice held a smile.

He took a deep breath and let it out slowly. "Unfortunately, I did not."

"No half-truths from you." Anna teased as she tried to hide her smile, with little success.

"Don't torment him, Anna. You know very well that he is beyond reproach. One must be willing to hear the truth when asking His Grace a question. It's one of the things for which he should be admired."

"Thank you, Mrs. Bainbridge." He dipped his head. "What was your question?"

"I asked if you chose the lovely bouquet to match the drawing room." Anna stared at her lap and straightened the tassel on her reticule.

"No. I didn't choose the flowers…" He stared at her.

Anna's head popped up. Disappointment was clearly marked on her face.

"To match the drawing room." He leaned forward. "I chose the flowers for what each bloom represents. The roses, yellow and peach represent sincerity and friendship. Sweet william symbolizes admiration and gratitude. And lavender is for purity and grace. Each attribute fits you quite well."

His words left Anna speechless. She peered at Mrs. Bainbridge, who gazed out the carriage window, seemingly enthralled by the scenery she had seen a hundred times.

"You mustn't say things like that. People may think you are courting me, Fraser."

He sat back. "How else can I thank you for your help? The sentiment is heartfelt." For a moment he thought to tease her, but he didn't want to spoil the moment.

"Each attribute fits you." He put a considerable amount of thought and time into choosing the flowers for her.

"Do you enjoy gardening, Your Grace?"

He turned to Mrs. Bainbridge. "Please, call me Willbury. Somehow—"

"You're still trying to grow into your title… Willbury."

He gave the headmistress a playful smile.

"That is one way to put it. Cutler startled me earlier. He always called me Master Fraser." He took a breath and for a moment let Anna and Mrs. Bainbridge experience his nostalgia. "As for gardening, I do enjoy it. There is an accomplishment, a joy in growing something from inception and seeing it blossom into maturity. I find it a way to escape the rigors of the courts."

"The flowers you brought are from your garden?" Anna stared at him with a new appreciation.

He had no idea why, but he wanted her to know he hadn't stopped at a flower stall at the marketplace and simply pointed to a bouquet. To him, it was important that she knew he put more thought into her gift.

"You've found me out, Anna. I moved several plants from my London rooms to the conservatory at The Willow. Yes, the flowers I brought you I picked earlier today from my garden."

The carriage stopped in front of The Rostov Tearoom. Willbury stepped out of the carriage and handed down the ladies.

"I need to stop at the modiste." Mrs. Bainbridge shook out her skirt, avoiding their gaze. "You two go on ahead. I'll be with you presently."

The headmistress looked at them, gave them a smile, and, without waiting for a response, made her way halfway down the street before Willbury and Anna gathered their wits. All they could do was stare at the retreating woman.

"So much for our chaperone." Willbury gestured toward the tearoom door. "Shall we?"

They stepped inside, and Willbury soaked up the familiar shop.

"Aunt Adelaide and I often came here for tea and her favorite ginger biscuits. I was eight years old the first time I invited her to tea and insisted I pay."

"Lady Anna. Your Grace. Welcome to the Tearoom." Tanya took off her apron and set off a small cloud of flour as she put the pinnie down on the counter.

Anna surveyed the dining room. An older couple sat at the only other occupied table.

"Have we arrived too early?" Willbury asked.

"Not at all. Others will be here soon enough. A table for two?"

"There will be three. Mrs. Bainbridge will be joining us."

"It's fortunate you came in today, Your Grace." Tanya led them to the other side of the room. "I just put the last tray of ginger biscuits into the oven."

"How would you know ginger biscuits are my favorite?"

"Mrs. Barton came in last week and mentioned you enjoyed them. I'll have tea and a plate of warm biscuits for three brought to your table."

Fraser helped her into her chair as Tanya made her way to the front of the tearoom. He turned to her with his irresistibly devastating grin.

Anna busied herself by removing her gloves and putting them into her reticule, then placing it on her lap all to avoid his gaze. When she could no longer stall, she raised her head and found him sitting across from her and still staring.

What should she say? It was as if she didn't know this man when they had been friends most of their lives. Well, she certainly didn't know him as a military man, a barrister, a duke, and especially not as someone courting her. The blood pounded in her ears. Her vision blurred. She had to get away. She couldn't stay near him a minute longer. She couldn't look at him. There was too much risk of him trying to talk her out of her decision. All she knew was the boy she'd grown up with, not the man who sat next to her; in a moment of panic, she wanted to leave.

"I didn't intend to embarrass you. I can't help the way I look at you." His elbow was on the table with his chin in his hand. "One glance and I find myself smiling."

He removed his hand and struck a more proper pose, opened his serviette, and draped it on his lap.

Was he playing his part? She glanced at the couple at the other table and concluded he was courting her for their sake. She took a long, slow deep breath. Perhaps she could play the game as well.

"You flatter me, Fraser." She gracefully placed her hand to her throat. "Or should I say you flatter yourself if you think I'm embarrassed." She sat up straighter and peered down her nose following propriety. For two Seasons she observed and learned as girls struck that position.

"Oh?" He dared to struggle to hide his chuckle.

"Ginger biscuits, really, Fraser. I would have thought you'd had your fill as a boy and moved on to other more tempting morsels."

He leaned closer toward her. His eyes were even more passionate than they had been moments before. He took her hand, and her breath caught.

"Oh, but I have moved on to a more tempting… morsel. Much more tempting. Would you like me to elaborate?" With that, he raised her hand.

Chapter Eight

She stared at her hand as he raised it. His eyes didn't leave hers as he brought her hand closer to his lips.

Her heart pounded, echoed in her ears. Surely her heart was going to jump out of her chest, yet still, she didn't move. She should pull her hand away, but she let him have it. By all that was holy, she waited. Waited. For him to…

His soft warm lips kissed the back of her hand.

Her eyes fluttered closed as a storm brewed inside her. One moment, she was chilled, and the next, she was warm in places she had never been warm before. She didn't want him to let go, break the connection, ever.

"The appropriate thing to do when a man meets a woman at social gatherings or otherwise"—his voice dropped to a warm, whiskey baritone—"is to kiss her hand to show respect, admiration, and devotion."

Fraser turned her hand over. Her eyelids flew open. They were alone in the middle of a haze. He still stared at her with eyes that held the answer to a mystery that she needed to solve. She struggled to keep a level head until he kissed her palm.

Dizzy with a gamut of emotions, one minute she wanted him to stop and the next she… the next she thought she would die if he did.

"Kissing the palm is different. This is an intimate statement without words, entirely inappropriate, but from the heart."

She shouldn't allow him to take such liberties. But at the moment, none of that mattered. At the moment, no one else in the tearoom mattered. At the moment, he and his tender kisses were all that mattered.

"Anna," he whispered.

She gazed into his eyes. Eyes filled with tenderness and passion. Swallowing hard, she wet her lips.

A low groan reached her ears as he lowered her hand to the table, released her, and sat back.

Anna didn't move. She couldn't if she wanted to. The space between them left her chilled and bereft. The tempest he set off that swirled inside her began to settle. In the distance, she recognized the sound of soft footsteps. Anna blinked and took a deep breath. The tearoom, which moments ago was a haze, came back into focus.

"Yes." The disappointment in her voice was palpable.

The server put down the tea pot and a plate of biscuits.

Fraser thanked the girl who hurried on her way. For a moment, he studied her intently. What weighed on him so heavily? Had he taken his game too far? There was no smugness about him. He looked as startled as she felt.

She poured tea and passed him his cup. Should she say something?

"Ginger biscuits." The voice behind them was low and deep.

He and Anna swung around. Both were surprised to see Mrs. Bainbridge and Lord Reese. They approached the table, and as they sat down, the world that moments ago had tilted in the most delightful way, righted itself, back to normal.

Fraser motioned to the server for another place setting.

"This is a pleasant surprise," Anna said to Lord Reese.

"Honoria insisted that I join you. She told me it was unlucky to have an odd number of people at a table. It only encouraged Mrs. Chernovsky to read your tea leaves to find you a happy ending."

The server brought over a place setting for Lord Reese.

"I had a lovely time last evening. Thank you for your hospitality." As Anna spoke, Fraser—no Willbury nodded in agreement and sipped his tea.

"I'm glad you both enjoyed the evening. I understand Willbury owes you a debt of gratitude, Lady Anna. You protected him all evening from the onslaught of merciless mothers eager to see their fledglings or sisters become the next Duchess of Willbury."

"He only says that because mothers have been after him as well." Mrs. Bainbridge gave Lord Reese a sideways glance.

"Ah, but I do not come with the prospect of making a woman a duchess. I leave that to my brother Edward. His answer to the problem of overenthusiastic mothers is to spend as much time as possible in

Parliament. To all, he is courting Lady Justice. To me, he is hiding. When he does venture out, he escorts the Dowager Countess of Calverton."

"Prudence Fleetwood?" Lord Reese put down his teacup at Willbury's shocked expression.

"The same. Why do you question his taste?" Lord Reese gave him a saucy grin.

Mrs. Bainbridge tapped his arm. "You must stop teasing them." She turned to Willbury and Anna.

"Lady Calverton is a dear friend of Lord Reese's family." Mrs. Bainbridge glimpsed at Barrington.

He stirred his tea, took a biscuit, and nodded his approval for her to continue.

"She's in her seventies and his brother enjoys her company. Lady Calverton enjoys being on Edward's arm."

"On another topic, will your brother be in Sommer-by-the-Sea a week from Sunday? Lady Anna is assisting me with preparing a reception. The three of us"—Willbury nodded at Mrs. Bainbridge—"decided it was the best way to introduce the newly titled duke. I would like to include him on the guest list."

Lord Reese put down his cup. "I do believe Edward will be here next week. He's coming to speak with Judge Scofield about the election. He has a concern about Saxton's opponent."

"The Home Office is concerned?" Anna gaped in amazement, first at Willbury, then at Lord Reese.

"Edward hasn't told me much. I suspect he wants to talk about campaign strategy. I'll know more after we speak with Scofield. Send his invitation to my residence. He stays with me when he visits the village."

"Excuse my intrusion, Barrington." The man clapped Lord Reese on the back. "It is good to see you."

The four raised their heads in unison. The occupant of the table across the room stood next to Lord Reese. A portly man, his clothes spoke of his success. His trousers and coat were stylish and made of a fine wool, but it was his waistcoat that caught the eye. The copper thread on cream satin was an intricately embroidered brocade pattern that included the monogram HS.

"Spivey." Lord Reese sat very still. The uncustomary critical tone in his voice rang in her ear.

"I didn't want to leave without saying hello." The man appeared affable except his smile didn't reach his eyes.

He had the audacity to stare at her. No, the man studied her. His probing glare looked her over, like a specimen in a laboratory.

"May I present the Duke of Willbury, Lady Marianna Ravencroft, and Mrs. Bainbridge. This is Mr. Harold Spivey."

"Ladies. It is my pleasure to meet you. His Grace"—he nodded to Willbury—"and I met in London. I was sorry to hear about your aunt. A fall down the stairs is unfortunate."

"A fall?" Anna gave Willbury a startled gaze.

"Oh, was that not public knowledge? I overheard the steward in the tavern. But I see you are having a private conversation. I won't bother you any longer." He nodded and returned to his table.

He didn't sit. Instead, the woman with him stood, and they both walked out of the tearoom.

"Who is that man?" Anna could not recognize his face, but she knew his name. He was Richard's sponsor.

"He is an industrialist. He's moved from London to Newcastle Upon Tyne. I don't know much about him. Mr. Bennett Sutton introduced me. I had dinner with Sutton in London when he and Judge Scofield were crafting Sutton's partnership agreement with the Duke of Blackhall." Willbury turned to the ladies. "How is Sutton's niece, Lady Katherine? Is she still working with him at the textile factory?"

"Not at the factory. She does all her work at her home," Mrs. Bainbridge said. "They're concerned the workers would walk out if they had any inkling a woman was involved with the machines. But that is another story."

"I'll make certain to add both Barrington brothers—the Duke of Oakdene and Lord Reese—to your list." Anna searched her reticule. She took out a pencil and rummaged for a piece of paper.

"I have the guest list right here." Willbury drew the list from his jacket pocket and handed it to Anna. "I didn't need to make many changes. I prefer you look it over. Feel free to add whomever you feel should be invited."

She opened the list, reviewed the names, and added Edward Barrington. She found Reese Barrington already listed.

"I am familiar with all these names except one." She raised her head and addressed Willbury. "Ellis Saxton. The name sounds familiar, but I can't place it."

"Judge Scofield suggested I include him. He is a bright young man from our borough who is campaigning for Parliament. He had written to me about a family matter last year. He introduced himself to me the day after I arrived here. He voiced his concerns for the farmers who have remained on the land as well as those people who are moving into cities like Sommer-by-the-Sea and Newcastle. You may have seen his name in the London papers." Willbury removed a pamphlet from his coat and put it on the table. "He's stated his political goals and explained how he plans to achieve them. It's all very well laid out."

"Yes, now I recall. Ellis Saxton, a well-spoken man with Whiggish ideas. I didn't realize he lived in our borough." Anna remembered the article. Her father had spoken about the young man one evening before her parents departed for Newcastle.

A cold chill ran up Anna's back. She picked up the pamphlet and read through it.

"Yes, refreshing progressive ideas, that is Saxton. He is well thought of by the others in the House of Commons, and he's viewed favorably by several in the House of Lords. I was impressed with his ideas and told him to see me if he needed help with his campaign. There is another seeking the same seat. Little is known about him, but Saxton has a long list of accomplishments."

Her cousin clearly told her the election was a formality, and he had no opposition. Richard's recent unease and desire for a bigger reception began to make sense.

"About Saxton's opponent." She placed her hand on his arm to get his attention. He had to know she was helping Richard.

He put his hand gently over hers. His touch silenced her as he continued talking to Lord Reese.

They supported different people. Perhaps she should withdraw from helping Fraser with his reception. If she didn't, and he found out another way, from another person, it would be embarrassing and would not go well.

There is no conflict between helping Fraser and Richard. The purposes driving each of the receptions are very different. No. There is no need to step away from either event., I still have to tell him. Privately. Not here.

She sat up straighter and removed her hand from his.

"I'm sure you remember the Saxtons." He turned to her, but all she did was smile. "Their farm is on the northside of The Willow. Ellis's older brother, Aunt Adelaide's steward, used to come to your defense when I teased you."

Anna popped to attention. "Lloyd? Yes, Lloyd Saxton. That's why the name sounded familiar. Lloyd came to a bad end. It must be eight years ago. He was accused of theft. They found the empty velvet coin pouch in

Lloyd's kit. Your aunt surprised everyone when she spoke in his defense. The incriminating evidence against him couldn't be denied. In the end, they sent him off to New South Wales."

"Lloyd proved to be a hard worker. After serving his sentence, he decided to stay in the new colony. He wrote home and told his family there were more opportunities for him there than in England. He still claims his innocence. It was Lloyd's story that spurred his brother Ellis's desire to serve in Parliament. Ellis has been writing to me. He found some interesting information about Lloyd's case and asked for my assistance."

"Do you think you can help him after so many years? So many people have moved away."

"I agree, Mrs. Bainbridge. I have an investigator looking for several people. He's questioned and gathered information from the four he found. I'm expecting his report presently."

"What information would survive after all this time? I've found that memories get cloudy and cannot be trusted."

Anna listened as Willbury answered Mrs. Bainbridge's questions. Her mind went back to Richard, Saxton, and the election. From everything she read in the pamphlet and what she remembered of Ellis Saxton, he would be an excellent choice for borough representative.

Richard must have known Saxton was running against him. And she thought he was lazy. Mrs. Cutler had warned her. How could she be so naïve?

The election was a formality. I am unopposed. What did he hope to gain by lying to her? What else did he conveniently overlook?

She built her business on trust and honesty. How could she support Richard now, family or not? She should have pressed him for more information about his platform.

"Willbury." Everyone turned toward her. Anna's momentary resolve to tell him everything fled, leaving her confused and angry with herself.

She and Willbury had a spark, a small one, but a spark nonetheless, and she wanted, no she needed to know if that spark could grow into a light for the future. Future? There was no way her dilemma would end well. She began to shiver as images of losing him built in her mind..

"Are you unwell?" Willbury leaned close.

"Why do you ask?" She straightened and lifted her cup, looking forward to sipping the warm brew, putting her hands around the cup to warm them.

He took her hand and stared at her as once again she shivered.

"You're trembling." The concern in his voice added to her anxiety.

"It's nothing." Her voice was a whisper.

He took off his jacket and placed it over her shoulders.

"Nonsense. I'll return you to Raven Hall. Mrs. Cutler will know what to do," Willbury said, his full attention on Anna.

"You take care of Lady Anna. I'll see Mrs. Bainbridge home."

"This is unnecessary. I am perfectly fine." Again, her shoulders shuddered.

"I will admit you are brave, but it is obvious you need some attention. Come, Mrs. Bainbridge. We'll leave Willbury to help Lady Anna." Lord Reese leaned close to Anna. "You have the best man taking care of you. I trusted him on the battlefield with my life."

Anna got to her feet. Mrs. Bainbridge went to her side.

"I know you're not ill. What's wrong? You used to shiver like this when you were a student. What made you upset? Did Willbury say or do anything?"

"Of course not. Except for a bit of teasing, he's been a perfect gentleman." Anna paused.

Go ahead, tell Mrs. Bainbridge. You know you can trust her. Anna took a deep breath.

"You know I am helping my cousin Richard. He is Saxton's opponent." She looked quickly at Willbury speaking with Lord Reese. "He went on and on about Saxton."

"Is that what has you all in a twist?" Mrs. Bainbridge took her hands. Anna raised her chin and looked at her. "It's perfectly fine to have differing political opinions."

"But we don't. I am obligated to help Richard because he is family. I cannot go back on my word, especially with the election only a few weeks away. I arrived without Willbury at the soiree last evening because I was working on the invitation list for Richard."

Mrs. Bainbridge stepped in front of her. "Listen to me, Anna. I admire your loyalty. But you should not compromise your beliefs and values for anyone. Willbury spoke of half-truths earlier, and how they turn into great lies. He was correct. I think this revelation has caught you by surprise. I am sure if you think about the situation, you will make the right decision."

"I must tell him, mustn't I?" The knot in her throat heated until she could hardly swallow. Half-truth. She didn't mentioned Richard's other lies.

Mrs. Bainbridge put her arm around her. "Yes, you do."

Chapter Nine

Fraser handed Anna into the coach, then took the seat next to her.

The silence was awkward and disturbing. Anna tried to think of something to say while she waited for the carriage to start off.

Say something. Anything.

"I didn't know Lord Reese liked ginger cookies." She closed her eyes. What a ridiculous remark. Why was it suddenly so difficult to speak her mind and to Fraser of all people? She'd never had a problem speaking her mind before. Her feelings were her own and she shouldn't have to worry about his opinions or hide them from anyone, especially him.

"I suppose ginger cookies are a reminder of his childhood. I believe certain food, music, even aromas bring back memories." His comment was factual, precise, but unemotional, and he stared either straight ahead at the blank seat across from them, or out the window at the town square.

She leaned toward him to be heard over the market noise.

"Do you know much about Mr. Spivey?"

He swung around and faced her. He was wound as tight as a woman laced in her corset. "Why do you ask?"

She drew back, her hand at her throat, stunned by his angry tone. Anna took a deep breath, not for air but to shore up her determination.

"Fraser. It was a civil question. Neither you nor Lord Reese think well of him. I asked a simple question."

"Forgive me, Anna. He didn't come to our table simply to say hello. That is not the man's character. He thinks himself superior to us and would never try to gain our favor. No. He came to our table for another reason.

One was to let me know how Aunt Adelaide died. That wasn't public knowledge. I wish I knew what he is up to." He drummed his fingers on the seat cushion. "Mr. Spivey is a businessman who dabbles in government and politics for his own gain, not for the welfare of the people he manages. I and one of the senior partners in my office, Mr. Lacey, met with him on a professional basis."

"I surmise you and Mr. Lacey weren't representing Mr. Spivey, but rather you were on the opposite side of the issue at hand."

Fraser "loosened his stays" and got more comfortable. His face transformed from what she expected was his stony business mask to the gentle man she knew.

"We did not agree on a point of law. He was very adamant and would not relent. Neither would Mr. Lacey or I. The law is the law. The last place I expected to encounter him was in a quiet tearoom in Sommer-by-the-Sea. But enough about Mr. Spivey. On to a more pleasant topic."

Anna was happy to close that discussion. Another opportunity to inform him would arise, definitely, before they reached Raven Hall.

"I hope you enjoyed our tea together. I certainly did. I think our arrangement is working quite well, don't you?

Anna rummaged in her reticule and drew out a piece of paper. "In my quest to protect you from overbearing mothers and their daughters, I thought of some women you might find acceptable. Rather than meeting them in public, I thought I could invite them to tea and introduce them to you."

"Possibly." His eyes that had been almost murderous a few heartbeats ago now brimmed with amusement.

Relieved, Anna settled in her seat.

"Since you do not have the need for a title or to enlarge your bank account, I chose women who come from the gentry. And yes, they benefit by marrying a man with a title, but these aren't simpering women. They are strong and independent. I think either one could make you a perfect… partner."

"I'm surprised. I can see you've given this a great deal of thought. I will have to put my mind to this and start a list of acceptable men for your hand. Now, who are these two title-seeking, strong, smart women?" He didn't try to hide the playfulness in his voice, and she felt a ripple of excitement.

"Catherine Holbeck and Hannah St. George. They are both lovely ladies."

Fraser's mouth opened into a perfect **o**. His hesitation had her instantly concerned.

He took a breath. "I've been introduced to one of those ladies at Almack's. Let me say I found her not to be someone I would pursue as a partner. As for the other…" He paused for a moment and stared at her. "Her family does not need my money. Several of them do need my services as a barrister. However, their issues aren't the type that I take on."

Anna sat next to him wide-eyed, her jaw dropped open. With his forefinger and a gentle touch, he lifted it closed as the carriage came to a stop.

Anna peeked out the window. They were in front of Raven Hall. The ride had gone by so quickly, and she hadn't told him about Richard. She dared not blurt it out, then walk away and leave him standing there. It would be better if they were comfortably inside, with a cup of tea. No, a glass of her father's brandy. Then she would tell him.

The driver opened the door. Fraser alighted, then helped her down. She shook out her skirts, and they started up the path toward the door.

"You will come in for a glass of Father's brandy."

"Would that I could, but I have an appointment that I can't postpone."

She was startled into silence when he declined her invitation.

He turned and stared into her eyes. After a moment, it couldn't have been longer than that, he took her hand. "I had no intention of boring you with Mr. Spivey and apologize if I upset you. But I have an appointment and cannot stay. This isn't the way I wanted to end our time together." He took a pamphlet out of his jacket pocket and handed it to her. "I wanted to mention this at tea. There is a discussion at the circulating library tomorrow about the book, *Waverly*. I thought you and Mrs. Bainbridge would enjoy the discussion. I hope you will join me."

They continued onto the porch. Mr. Cutler was more than efficient. He opened the door as they reached the porch.

"I would very much enjoy going to the discussion with you."

He gave her a broad smile, and for a moment, he looked like an awkward boy.

"I will collect you and Mrs. Bainbridge at 11:00 tomorrow morning." He took her hand and kissed it tenderly.

"Your Grace—"

He shook his head and waited.

"Fraser, thank you for the lovely flowers and for an enjoyable afternoon. I'm looking forward to tomorrow."

"My pleasure, Anna. Until tomorrow." He returned to his waiting carriage.

Anna watched as the carriage reached the end of the drive and turned onto King's Way. She would tell him about Richard tomorrow.

"What has you preoccupied? You haven't listened to a thing I've said." Willbury and Barrington sat in Judge Scofield's office around a table.

"He's preoccupied either by the lovely Lady Anna Ravencroft or the nefarious Harold Spivey." Barrington's playful smirk landed on a conflicted Willbury.

"Actually, both have distracted me. I intended to have a quiet, pleasant tea with Lady Anna and Mrs. Bainbridge. You, Barrington, were an added delight."

Barrington nodded with a smile.

"We could have done without Harold Spivey. He didn't walk across the tearoom to say hello to us. I don't know why he came over. I'm puzzled about how he knew the circumstances around Aunt Adelaide's death. It's bedeviling me."

"And you have a sensible reason for concern." Judge Scofield's voice wasn't loud but still commanded their attention. "Spivey has been identified as the man behind the politically unknown young men campaigning for Parliament in various boroughs. He's doing more than sponsoring them. It would be one thing if these were men who wanted to fulfill their civic duty. They are not. From what I've learned, when asked about their political position, each of them parrots the same rehearsed statement, verbatim. Not a word is added or omitted. No. Spivey is hand-picking men he can control."

"This is why Edward is visiting us here." Barrington's playful smirk was gone.

"It's also why I have one of my staff looking into the background of each person campaigning in the rotten boroughs as well as their associates." Scofield jabbed at the table with each word. "At the same time, I have a team looking into Spivey's background."

Barrington moved forward in his chair and faced Willbury. "That brings us to why we wanted to speak to you."

Willbury turned to him. "I'm listening."

"Your estate is in one of the boroughs. Ellis Saxton is campaigning there. He is the type of man we all want in Parliament." Barrington handed him a pamphlet he hadn't seen before.

Willbury's lips curled into a snarl. He tossed the offending document onto the table, unable to get it out of his hands fast enough.

"I cannot believe that any of these ridiculous claims are true. This rubbish is misleading, half-truths, and, in some cases, whole lies." Willbury pointed at the offending document on the table. "There is no talk about the needs of the people in the borough. This is nothing more than a personal attack on Saxton."

"Our thoughts as well." Barrington sat back.

"You may know the man who is in Newcastle handling the investigation for me. He's one of Barrington's men, James Wilmore," the judge said. "According to him, none of the incidents referenced in the document are true. Saxton never married. He never had children, much less abandoned them. Nor was he responsible for his brother's exile to New South Wales. There is speculation that Francis Younge's son, Richard, may run against him."

"Younge has been a member of Parliament for as long as I can remember. He sent me a letter of congratulations when I inherited the title. He mentioned he was retiring and campaigning diligently for Saxton. He made no mention of his son."

"There is a big gathering being planned that will formally announce Spivey's choice for Parliament in your borough. As the Duke of Willbury and a voting resident of the borough, your favorable endorsement and generous funding would be desirable. We suspect you may be invited to attend."

"Barrington, you don't have to ask for my help." Willbury looked from one man to the other. "You know you have it. I didn't think my activities as a barrister would be needed, especially in local politics."

Scofield poured his guests a splash of whiskey and handed them each a glass. "Then we are in agreement. To put a stop to Spivey and his plans."

They raised their glasses and drank to seal their pledge.

The smoky aroma and the sharp bitter taste that was fine whiskey slid down his throat. He downed it quickly.

"If you will excuse me." Willbury set down his empty glass. "I planned to go to Newcastle today. I have several people I want to see. I'll include Wilmore. It will be good to see him again."

Willbury rode toward The Willow leaving all thoughts of the judge, Barrington, the upcoming election, and Spivey behind.

His mind was filled with Anna. He played the courting lover but soon realized there was more behind his display of affection.

He and Anna had exchanged letters regularly when he first left Sommer-by-the-Sea. He had looked forward to reading her messages. But after his first six months on active duty, the tone of his writing changed. Every letter he drafted had been filled with the war, what he he'd seen, and worse, what he had done. He had censored everything he wrote, rereading, crossing out, destroying pages. He'd come away frustrated and angry. Finally, he had given up writing to her. He couldn't offer her anything positive, anything pleasant. There had been no future, not in that awful place with death and the dying all around him. Thoughts of her hadn't belonged there. To keep her safe, he had banned her from his mind.

He chuckled. After all these years, he thought he had moved on, and Anna was safely behind that big wall. He ran his hand through his hair. Today, he realized his feelings for her were still there. They had never gone away.

When he kissed her hand, he expected a reprimand, but when he gazed into her eyes, they mirrored the truth. Her truth. At first, he thought he had gone too far, but... it grew naturally, truthfully. They both felt the strong attraction. He understood exactly what the feeling meant. So did she.

He was daring in the tearoom. Perhaps she was being kind, not wanting to cause a scene. That thought was amusing. Anna wouldn't make a scene, but she wouldn't hesitate to put him in his place either. There was something deeper here, and the last thing he wanted was to scare her away. No. He couldn't let that happen.

Half-truths would not do, especially in a relationship with Anna. She deserved the whole truth. He couldn't change any of the past. There were things he couldn't tell her, not yet. When he did, she would have to decide for herself. Until then, he had to provide her with reasons that he was acceptable to her. A broad grin blossomed across his face. Court her. Really court her and make her fall in love with him. Then he would tell her everything. He wasn't sure how to tell her, but he was certain he would know when the time was right.

He urged his horse to a canter and went on to Newcastle.

Chapter Ten

It was early in the day, but Anna already had a busy morning. She secured the circulating library for Richard's event, and the last of Willbury's invitations were written and delivered. The stack of invitations to Richard's reception waited on her desk for the location of the event to be added. The morning mail sat to the side, waiting for her to review.

Anna fidgeted with Richard's guest list. Her mind was miles away as she reviewed the list without remembering a single name she had read. She returned the document to her desk. One moment, she was upset about what she learned about Richard, and the next, it was the leering grin of Mr. Spivey.

She went over the encounter with the sponsor several times, and with each iteration, she arrived at the same conclusion. He had directed his calculating stare at her. She had received similar attention at Almack's. Spivey didn't admire her long brown hair, turned-up nose, her quick wit, or her skill at the piano. Spivey, like her would-be-suitors, admired her bank account.

Anna stared at the disaster that was the preliminary guest list. Titled, gentry, farmers, and workers all mixed together for a seated dinner. Of the eighty people on this list, only fifteen voted in this borough.

By all that is holy. She picked up a piece of mail. She would not be surprised if the event turned volatile.

She picked up the letter opener. Her thoughts were interrupted by a single tap on the door.

"Come."

"Mr. Younge, my lady." Mr. Cutler stood to the side as Richard entered.

She slit open the letter and put on a smile although, at the moment, Richard was the last person she wanted to see.

"Good morning. I'm here to deliver the invitations for you. I know Cutler has other things to do."

He looked at her desk. "Have they already been delivered?"

"No. I cannot put my name or open my home to what you propose." She didn't look at him but rather read the note.

"Anna—"

She glared at Richard, the letter opener poised in her hand.

"And please, don't tell me I've promised your father. The guest list is inappropriate. I will not be part of creating conditions for a brawl. As for having your reception here, it is unfortunate, but my house is not available. That said, I have secured the circulating library where the variety of people can congregate as they see fit. It will be a light menu, and you will, of course, prepare a speech."

He listened with a blank stare. He was taking this better than she expected.

"You will need to choose someone to introduce you. I suggest the Lord Mayor. Since your guest list is all gentlemen, and the event is in a public place, I will not be attending."

She finished and waited for him to say something. He stared at the floor as if the answer was somehow hidden in the pattern of the carpet. After several moments, he nodded, apparently coming to some conclusion.

"I understand. I have a tendency to be overenthusiastic. It is a trait I must work on. I hope you will not hold it against me. Give me a chance to regain your trust. Not right now. You are right. The guest list was not realistic, and assuming the reception would be here is unforgivable." He put his hand over his heart.

He went to her side and pulled her to her feet.

"I brought you a token of my appreciation. For all you have done. I had planned to give it to you at the reception, but whether you attend or not, I still want you to have it."

He removed a small box from his pocket and put it in her hand.

"I thought of you when I saw this. Fate told me it was yours when I turned it over."

She stared at him, then the box. He nodded, encouraging her to open his gift.

She pulled the red ribbon that held the black leather box closed. Anna didn't know what to expect. She opened the top and was stunned.

A diamond pendant sat in the dark-blue, velvet-lined box. The bail was flower shaped with a diamond set into each of the five petals. Beneath it hung a drop. The center stone was a clear blue-white oval diamond embellished with smaller stones around it.

Anna was speechless.

He reached into the box and turned the pendant over. Engraved into the back were the letters AR and the words *Mon bijou. Mon Coeur*, My jewel, my heart.

"Richard. This is lovely. More than lovely, but I cannot accept this." She closed the box and tried to hand it back to him.

"No. It is for you." He held up his hands and stepped back.

"Richard. I will not accept this. It is not a gift for a friend doing you a favor."

"Think of this as a token of my feelings for you. I thought we could be much more than friends." He took the box, put it on her desk, and held her hands. "I don't expect you to answer me right away."

She pulled her hands loose from his.

"Richard. I can see your offer is heartfelt, but I must tell you I do not feel the same way as you do."

"Then it's true. It's Willbury? You know nothing will come of that."

Did she hear him correctly? Her thoughts stuttered for a moment, and with widened eyes, every part of her paused while her mind caught up.

"His display in the tearoom was, well I can't say I was surprised that he would take such liberties, but I never expected your name to be associated with him. Frankly, I thought better of you. You know you cannot see him again if you want to keep your good name.

"Are you aware of his reputation in London? I know he is a longtime friend, but people change. Sometimes it is not for the best. I shouldn't be telling you this. It's not for a lady's ears, but you must understand I am trying to protect you."

Anna stared at him, unable to speak.

"While he was in the service, he socialized with the enemy, a female spy, while his friends, the men he fought with, died. And there was a child. He did not bring them with him when he returned."

All the warmth in her body drained away, leaving her chilled. Lies. This couldn't be true. Fraser would never.

"He may very well have been involved in the death of his…" He assumed a painful expression. "His brother."

"I know it's difficult to hear such distasteful things about someone you admire and trust. You know I am right. You'll thank me after you've had time to think about it. After you came home from your last Season in London, I was certain something was amiss. Now I know why you had no offers. Fate. We are destined for each other, no one else. Trust me. I will guide you in all things."

His accusations were absurd. Fraser didn't turn his back on his brother or his men. With abrupt clarity, she saw Richard for what he was, a manipulator and liar. She went to her desk and rang for Mr. Cutler, grabbed Richard's guest list, the gift from her desk, and shoved them at him.

"It would be best if you leave."

He stared at the papers and box in his hand, then at her. He tilted his head and assessed her from the hem of her skirt, to the clasp in her hair, and everything in between with an air of amusement. What did he know that she didn't?

Mr. Cutler entered. He stood next to Younge.

"Mr. Younge is leaving."

Richard ignored the butler. He let out a heavy sigh.

"We'll talk again. You'll see that I'm right." He placed the box back on her desk. With the list crushed in his hand, he left the room. Mr. Cutler close behind him.

"How did this happen?" Anna murmured as she shook her head and fell into the seat at her desk.

"For your family."

She turned to see Mrs. Cutler at the door with her pelisse in her hand.

"Willbury will be here presently."

Anna took out a piece of paper, quill, and ink.

"Ask Mr. Cutler to have this delivered to my father. He's still in Newcastle."

Her brief note complete, she blotted, folded, and handed it to her housekeeper. Anna stood as her housekeeper helped her with her pelisse.

"Have them wait for an answer."

Mrs. Cutler nodded and put the note in her pocket.

"Do you want to ban him from the house?"

Anna's arm in one sleeve, she hesitated before she continued.

"Thank you, no. But it is a thought. I have never in my life thrown anyone out of this house. He had some nerve to speak against Fraser, telling me the most insidious lies." She turned and faced the woman. "Then he had the audacity to propose."

"There are rumblings that Willbury is courting you. The only way your cousin can compete is to insinuate that Willbury will compromise your good name." The housekeeper shook her head as she straightened Anna's skirt. "Richard Younge doesn't see you for who you are. He sees your money and how fast he can spend it."

Anna stood looking out the window.

"He accused Fraser of being a traitor, having and abandoning a child, and being involved in his brother's death. Furthermore, he insinuated I needed someone like him to take care of me. I declined his proposal and withdrew my support for his campaign."

"My lady." Mr. Cutler stood at the door.

"Yes?" A warning set her off. Had Richard caused a scene?

"The Duke of Willbury."

The butler and his wife withdrew.

Fraser took no more than three steps into the room when his expression grew serious. He hurried to her side. He didn't say anything. He stood next to her. They gazed out at the garden together.

"Is there anything you'd like to talk about?" His warm, low voice cut through her thoughts.

Yes, there was, but not now. Instead, she shook her head. "It's a private matter. The other person was more disappointed than me."

"If you need someone to talk to, you know you can depend on me." He turned to her. "Would you like to play a game of cards rather than go to the library? I'll let you win. We can attend the theater tonight if you like."

"That would be lovely. But you won't have to let me win. I used to trounce you when we played cards."

"Ah, but I've learned a great deal since then."

He took her hand and gently kissed her knuckles. They stood for several more minutes enjoying the garden. She gave him a sideways glance.

How could anyone believe the vile things Richard professed?

Chapter Eleven

Willbury whistled as he transversed the field, taking a faster route back to The Willow from Raven Hall. The trek brought back memories of his younger years. He took a deep breath, the smells of autumn all around him, not the warm apple tarts he pilfered when he was younger. His step was light, and his mind was clear as he went on.

Anna was determined to find him an acceptable life partner. While they played whist, she had presented two more candidates. Their pedigrees were impeccable. Their attributes were admirable. Their accomplishments were impressive. He thanked her for her efforts and told her neither caught his interest.

"Why? They are lovely young ladies."

"I am sure both come from fine, proud families." He stared at his cards as he contemplated what he should say but was unwilling to show his hand.

He was sure they were lovely ladies, but not like Anna. The women were trustworthy, but not like Anna. The women were accomplished. They, too, played whist, but he was certain they didn't play with as much daring as Anna. No, they couldn't compare to her.

They played four games. She handily outplayed him in the first and third games. He could still see her head thrown back laughing when she outsmarted him, and how she graciously lost the second and fourth hands to him.

He was about to suggest a fifth to break the tie when two of her friends arrived for tea.

"Lady Euphemia, Lady Harriet, may I present the Duke of Willbury? He is the great-nephew of the late Duchess of Willbury. Your Grace, Lady Euphemia Brandt, and Lady Harriet Manning. Both are dear friends of mine. We attended Mrs. Bainbridge's seminary together."

"Your Grace, I was so sorry to hear of your aunt's passing," Lady Euphemia had said.

"Thank you, ma'am, I appreciate your kind words."

"Her Grace was a warm, loving, and generous woman."

"Thank you, Lady Harriet. And she had a wicked sense of humor. I do miss that. How is your father? I became acquainted with him in London when he administered to Barrington. You must have missed his services here in Sommer-by-the-Sea."

"Besides being an excellent surgeon, my father is a superb teacher. I took over his responsibilities with Anna's help."

Lady Harriet stepped in for her father? The woman is just as unpredictable as Anna and was proud of it. His eyes met hers. A flash rushed to her face. He thought she would turn to a cinder.

"Please give him my regards. Now ladies, if you will excuse me."

"I hope you aren't leaving on our account." Lady Harriet had glanced at the others next to her.

"Not at all. Lady Anna has trounced me well at whist. I need time to recuperate."

"Come." Anna had stepped forward. "I'll see you to the door."

She'd swept out of the room with him, leaving her surprised friends behind.

"I didn't know you were a nurse. It seems I have a lot to learn about you." He took his hat from Mr. Cutler and held it up so the butler couldn't see them, kissed her forehead, then put on his hat. "I'll arrange for supper to be served after the theater. Mrs. Bainbridge and Barrington will be joining us."

"That will be lovely." She had paused for an awkward moment. "You have my appreciation for—"

"There's no need to say anything. I had a much better morning playing cards with you than listening to a lecture. I didn't have to share you with anyone else." The butler opened the door. "I'll collect you at 5:30. Tonight's performance is *The Merchant of Venice*. It's a favorite of mine. We're especially fortunate. Edmund Kean is traveling to Edinburgh and is stopping in Sommer-by-the-Sea on his way and has agreed to perform."

Anna had been in a better state of mind than when he found her. For that he was glad. But what had someone said or done that made her so upset?

♥ ♥ ♥

A message waited for him on the salver in the hall upon his arrival home. He took it with him into his library.

> *My source confirmed one of the candidates we discussed has empty pockets. He is not backed by the current MP and lost his benefactor in August. A new sponsor now funds him and recently called in the debt. Without immediate repayment, the sponsor will not extend any additional funds. The election is four weeks away.*

He folded the message.

"Excuse me, Your Grace."

Willbury looked up to see Mr. Barton at the door. "Richard Younge."

Richard walked into the library, his hat in his hand.

"Willbury. I wanted to reestablish our acquaintance. It's been some time since we've seen each other. I'm here to extend my condolences on the passing of your aunt and speak to you about my borough."

Willbury overlooked the informal nature of his greeting. He knew Richard, albeit from a distance. He was the thorn in everyone's side during their youth. He arrived at places uninvited and disrupted everything, making him a *persona non grata*.

Richard and Lucian had been adversaries. Lucian was younger by thirty minutes, and while they were identical twins, he was not as outspoken as Fraser. What he didn't have in bravado he'd made up for in strength and cunning. Against Lucian, Richard never had a chance.

Willbury gestured to the chairs in front of the hearth.

Kaiah padded into the room and went directly to Willbury. Sitting beside him on her haunches, she came up to Willbury's shoulder. The dog's penetrating, wise, wolf-like eyes, had a gentleness that reflected a noble heart. Kaiah stared unblinking at Younge.

Younge, uncomfortable in front of the dog, said nothing. From the sweat beading on his forehead, he didn't have to say a word.

At first, Willbury thought he was hearing things until he stroked the dog. Kaiah's rumbling, deep growl caught him off guard. He paid close attention to every movement Younge made.

The man nervously stared at Kaiah, ready to spring from his chair. It wasn't a fear of animals. It was the fear of *this* animal. It was unlike Kaiah to take a dislike to anyone. He kept a comforting hand on the dog.

"I am replacing my father as the next borough representative. I am calling on every voter in order for them to put a face to my name. It is strange seeing you here. I thought I would be sitting with Her Grace, who was always interested in what I did. She supported and encouraged me to devote myself to the same career as my father."

"Very admirable. Francis's devotion to his constituency during his time in service is more than admirable. Over the years, the political landscape has changed, as has the population distribution. This district is a prime example. Many have abandoned their farms and sheep for the factories in the city. This borough consists of little more than five farms and an estate. There are fifteen people eligible to vote, but the borough also contains laborers, factory owners, and workers as well as the village shop owners and families." Willbury shifted in his chair.

Kaiah sprang to her feet.

He silently signaled her to sit. The dog obeyed.

"I understand that Ellis Saxton is campaigning for borough representative as well. He told me his position. How is it different from yours?"

Richard, who hadn't taken his eyes off the dog, moved his attention to Willbury. "I will gladly tell you in great detail. However, I am here to invite you to my reception on the fourth of October, the day before voting begins. That is where I will disclose everything."

"Thank you. I assure you I will consider attending. Where is it being held?"

"I am a bit premature with my invitation." Younge gave his next remark great thought. "My fiancée and I are in discussions. She is adamant that she hosts the reception, and I'm not certain it is appropriate. We haven't announced our intentions. You can expect the invitation presently."

Willbury translated that to mean he's trying to convince the poor girl into marrying him and hosting an event that is way beyond her ability.

"Congratulations on your good fortune." Willbury stood, signaling the visit was over.

Younge got to his feet.

His visitor turned pale when the dog stood with his ears forward. Kaiah definitely had an issue with Younge. He wondered what it was.

"Thank you for your time. I must be off. I'll see myself out." Younge couldn't hurry out the door fast enough. He heard the door slam shortly afterward.

"I didn't like him much either." Willbury gave Kaiah a good rub, still trying to connect the dog's reaction to Younge. "Come, we are both in need of a walk. And a good game of fetch."

Kaiah followed him through the adjoining drawing room and out the patio door. They passed the stable and went into the field beyond.

He threw a stick and Kaiah rushed off. Her muscles bunched and stretched as she covered the ground. She slowed down, turned, and jumped, catching the stick in her jaws. She trotted back to his side and dropped the stick at his feet.

"Good, girl. Ready for another?" He pulled his arm back ready to throw but stopped.

Kaiah lost all interest in their game. Her head up and her ears pointing forward, Kaiah took off toward the stable, barking as if a wolf was after the sheep.

Willbury hurried after her. He rushed into the stable and found Kaiah's teeth bared, growling at Younge.

"Heel."

The dog stood down and sat at Willbury's feet.

"Mr. Younge, what are you doing in my stable? I assure you we only have mares. There are no voters in here."

"I thought I'd say hello to Mr. Forbes." A flustered Richard took out his handkerchief and wiped his forehead. His eyes never left the animal. "The next thing I knew, the dog was growling at me."

"You'd best be going. I'll let Mr. Forbes know you asked after him."

"Yes." Younge hurried out of the building and headed east.

Willbury and Kaiah didn't move. He watched the retreating figure until he was certain his caller was gone this time.

Kaiah swiveled her head toward the house. Willbury followed her glance.

Mr. Forbes came down the path from the kitchen garden, taking the last bite of an apple tart and wiping his mouth with a handkerchief.

"You had a visitor, Mr. Forbes."

"Mrs. Barton told me Mr. Younge was here. If you don't mind me saying, I'm glad I missed him." He stuffed the cloth in his pocket.

"Do you know the man?" Willbury stared at Forbes. A warning voice whispered in his ear.

"Your Grace, Younge was the estate steward here for a few months. He did not make many friends among the staff."

"When was this?" How did he not know? He searched his mind, trying to find where he had missed that information.

"He began soon after the late duke passed on and stayed until the beginning of August, a few weeks before Her Grace's passing."

"I wasn't aware of his employment here." Willbury turned to leave but hesitated. "Mr. Forbes, Kaiah has a good disposition. Do you know any reason why she would get overly upset?"

"Her breed doesn't have aggressive tendencies, but she is a loyal and protective animal. She doesn't bark at everything she sees. When she does get upset, she barks loud enough to bring the walls down."

"When was the last time you heard her bring the walls down?"

"When you arrived, Your Grace."

"I hope that was a happy bark and not aggressive." Willbury and Forbes both chuckled.

"You could count the times she's gotten upset on one hand. The last time she went wild barking was the night the duchess passed away. We heard her but couldn't find her. We thought she was caught or something. One of the footmen found her closed up in Her Grace's closet."

"Closet?"

"Kaiah stayed in Her Grace's room at night."

"Yes, I know. She was very attached to my aunt." He ruffled Kaiah's head. "She was an excellent companion."

"We all thought the duchess must have accidently closed the dog in her closet before she started for the stairs."

Again, Willbury started for the main house and hesitated. "Where did Younge stay when he was the estate steward?"

"To his disappointment, he stayed in the steward's cottage." Forbes pointed to the west side of the field.

"Disappointment? I would think he would enjoy the cottage."

"You can ask Mr. Barton. Younge came on as the temporary estate steward supposedly for three months. He wanted to stay in the main house, but Her Grace told him the cottage or nothing."

"That sounds like my aunt."

"As far as I'm concerned, he could have lived in the stable. He told us over and over his father was a member of Parliament. It's my understanding that the only reason he was here was because his father sent Her Grace a letter with a request to take him on."

"Did Younge come to the stable often?"

"Not at all. If he wanted a horse, he sent one of the footmen."

Willbury nodded and stepped into the tack room where Kaiah had confronted Younge.

Forbes came up behind him. "Is there something you're looking for, Your Grace?"

"I cannot think of any reason why Younge came in here. He said he wanted to see you, but you have no relationship with him. So why did he come into the tack room?" He assessed the room, but all he saw were saddles, saddle racks, bridles, stirrups, reins, halters, bits, a pile of blankets, and storage chests.

"Mr. Forbes, I'd like you to empty all three storage chests and look for anything that's missing or doesn't belong there. When you're done, let me know if you find anything. This may lead to nothing."

"I understand. It shouldn't take long."

"Thank you. I'll have Mr. Barton send you some help." Willbury headed for the main house, the dog trotting beside him.

The more he thought about Younge's visit, the more certain he was that his visit wasn't to introduce himself. He stood at the doorway to the house and glanced back at the stable. He shook his head.

"Mr. Barton." Willbury bellowed as he walked down the hall to his library.

"Yes, Your Grace." The man came out, shrugging into his coat, a silver polishing cloth in his hand.

"Send someone out to assist Forbes in the stable, then come see me."

Barton nodded and returned quickly.

"What can you tell me about Mr. Younge? I understand he was the estate steward. I wouldn't think he'd be qualified."

"Temporary estate steward. He had been the assistant to the steward eight years ago." The butler spit out the words. Barton didn't like Younge either.

"Did anyone get along with Younge?"

"Not at all. He had no idea what he was doing. Mrs. Barton oversees the household accounts. He took them from her and made a mess of them. She was forever trying to straighten them out."

"What else?"

"The lower house maid found small pieces of art along with some silver and crystal missing. Her Grace sent the upper house maid to clean the cottage and found them decorating the cottage. The next time she went to clean they were gone. Soon after that, the staff removed anything that was removable and put the items in storage. And we began the inventory."

"Sit down, Mr. Barton. Tell me what you have found, or rather what you have found missing."

Chapter Twelve

Two hours later, Willbury had a comprehensive list of artworks, silver, family relics, and jewels for which no one could account.

"We were led to believe that Her Grace had given the pieces away."

"By Younge, no doubt."

"When I approached the subject, he told me to watch my words. He said the staff were in for a rude awakening. It was the other way around. He was quite irate when Judge Scofield excluded him when the will was read. Younge had the audacity to think Her Grace would leave him money, even the estate. He didn't know there was anyone who had a claim, certainly not you."

Willbury tried to suppress a chuckle but instead dissolved into stomach-shaking convulsions as he fought waves of laughter.

"He never did understand our family connections. He would ask, and no one would tell him. Eventually, he thought I was one of the local village boys." He wiped his eyes from laughing so hard. "He wants all this, and I want none of it. Well, we were both in for a grand surprise."

"If that will be all?" Mr. Barton got up.

"Yes. And thank you for the information. I do have one other question. Why did he leave at the beginning of August?"

"He presented a note to the duchess from his father. Francis Younge was promoting him to be the representative from the borough, and he needed to step away from his position to campaign. All the correspondence is in the estate files."

"Thank you for your help."

Willbury headed for the conservatory, mulling over what Barton and Forbes had told him.

"Pardon me, Your Grace. I didn't realize you were here." Mrs. Barton started to leave.

"No, come in. I was looking for flowers to bring to Lady Anna."

Mrs. Barton peered at what he was eyeing.

"I think a nosegay of violets and white tea roses would be nice. It would match the lavender gown she plans to wear tonight."

"Are you conspiring with me?" Willbury stared in disbelief at the woman.

"I certainly am. You go ahead and get dressed. I'll have the nosegay ready before you leave."

He went up the stairs. He passed his aunt's bedchamber and decided to step inside. Opening the door, he was taken by the darkness. It was a foolish notion that the room would be as it was with Aunt Adelaide in residence. She kept the curtains open to enjoy the light, whether sunlight or moonlight. Now the dark, empty room shouted that his aunt was gone.

There was a sadness in seeing the things she loved standing idle and forgotten. He lit a taper and ventured inside. Dust covers were over the furniture and bed. The armoire was empty. Not even a button. Deep scratches on the inside of the door attested to Kaiah trying to get out.

He walked across the room toward the small bookcase on the far wall. As he got closer, the taper's flame flickered. Curious, he moved the candle along the wall and halted at a spot where the candlelight flickered so that the flame almost went out.

More intrigued, he ran his hand along the top wainscotting and touched a piece of metal. He released it and, with a gentle touch, pushed the wall. The jib door opened.

A plume of dust belched, giving the air a musty smell. He stepped inside, brushed away the cobwebs, and stood in a narrow hall. The old servant's hall. The warren of halls and staircases had been closed off years ago, following the tragic death of an upstairs maid who fell down the stairs while carrying the breakfast of the duchess of the 5th Duke of Willbury.

The layer of dust, a depressing dirty gray, was thick on the floor. His eyes focused on an anomaly—footprints. From the size and shape, they were made by a man. Not recent ones. These were already being claimed by the surrounding dust.

He raised the candle. There were no other footprints. He carefully followed the tracks. They led to the central servants' steps. Here the lighting was somewhat better. A large skylight kept the servants' way well lit during the day. He could see that the staircase went up at least two, if not three floors, and down two.

Following the tracks, he went to the lowest level, then turned down a small hallway that branched off at an angle, away from the house. It was colder here. He wasn't in a hall but rather an earth tunnel.

He ventured a guess that this path led to the icehouse although he didn't see any handcarts or ice tools. At last, he came to a door. Expecting it to be locked, he pushed it and was surprised when it sprang open.

Bombarded by bright light, he stepped inside and squinted, trying to make out where he was. Moments later, he stared at Forbes, his face washed blank with confusion. The man's mind had a hard time reconciling who stood in front of him. Forbes stared at the jib door, then back at him.

"Your Grace?" The color was coming back to the man's face.

"I am just as surprised as you. I expected to walk into the icehouse." Willbury closed the door and stared at the horse blankets that hung on it. "Who would expect a servant's entrance in the stable?"

Forbes examined the device. "This is better than the ones in the house. If I didn't see you close the door, I would say there wasn't one here."

"The tunnel continues." Willbury looked out into the stable yard. "To the west."

"The only building on the estate in that direction is the steward's cottage. It's just over the rise."

"Interesting." Willbury took down the blankets and found an old, rusted slide latch. He opened the door and stepped inside.

"Your Grace? I'll go with you."

They followed the tunnel along for some time without finding any other outlets. They found old bottles, some broken tools, and other debris that they had to navigate, but more of an annoyance than of any consequence. They kept moving along. He was determined to see where this led and who had free access to The Willow.

"Your Grace? This is too well wrapped to be debris." Forbes handed him the small package.

Weighing it in his hand, he gave his head groom a questioning look then carefully unwrapped the bundle. They stared at a small silver tea pot.

"What's Her Grace's teapot doing in this mess?" Forbes gaped at the treasure.

"I wish I knew." Willbury peered down the tunnel and put the piece down.

They continued until they reached the end and faced a door. This one wasn't locked, either. With great care, Willbury opened it and stepped out. Forbes was right behind him. They found themselves in the hallway of the steward's cottage.

"You stay here. I'll be right back." Willbury made a quick reconnaissance of the small cottage. Satisfied it was empty and locked, he went back to the Forbes. "I don't need to see anything else."

Willbury was getting a better picture of what had happened at The Willow. The steward wasn't incompetent or overwhelmed. He was scheming and plotting,

Forbes followed him out, then turned, and locked the door. "No sense letting anyone in who we don't want."

"My thoughts, exactly."

Willbury had been in many tunnels during the war where secrets were passed, but he never thought he'd find one here. He picked up the teapot, and they retraced their steps until they came to the door of the tack room.

"You go in and lock the door. I'm going to my aunt's suite."

Forbes nodded.

Willbury waited until he heard the latch slide into place. Satisfied everything was secure, he went to the servants' stairs and sealed off the house from the stable and the steward's cottage.

He retraced his steps to his aunt's room, searching for anything that would indicate Younge had been here. There was nothing on the walls, and all he found on the floor were footprints and spots of candle drippings. He stood at the jib door, taking in his surroundings. Deep in his bones, he knew Younge had entered the house through this door. All he had to figure out was why and when.

At the moment, he had to dress for the evening. Setting the lock on the door and replacing the teapot on the table, he hurried on to his room. He was on his own this evening. His valet, Riley, was packing up the last of his things in London and wouldn't arrive until tomorrow.

He dressed and tried to tie his cravat. He'd done it a hundred times. Tonight, because he wanted it to be perfect, the cloth would not cooperate. Finally, he gave up in frustration.

Downstairs, Mrs. Barton met him at the door with the nosegay.

"Excuse me, Your Grace." She handed him the flowers and gestured to his cravat. "May I?"

"Oh, please, Mrs. Barton. This is the wrong time for Riley to be away."

"I would not let you out if you weren't perfect." In a moment, she was done. She stood back and admired her work. "Your carriage is ready."

"I would kiss you, Mrs. Barton, but Mr. Barton might call me out."
He nodded at his butler, who smiled from the doorway.

Since seeing Richard Younge this afternoon, his priorities had shifted.
Footprints, servant's stairs, and jib doors filled his mind along with trying
to understand their connections. As the carriage turned down the Raven
Hall drive, he cleared his mind, determined to enjoy Anna and the evening.
There was plenty of time to deal with Younge and the election.

He alighted from the carriage at Raven Hall and waited in the drawing
room with the small bouquet.

Chapter Thirteen

Anna stared in the looking glass. The lavender gown looked so different on her than it did on the hanger. She sparkled from the fine sheen of her silk petticoat, to the silver threads, and a scattering of seed pearls on her lace overskirt. Mrs. Cutler put her hair up with seed pearls cleverly placed.

She swept into the drawing room.

"Everyone's eyes will be on you and not Edmund Kean." He gave her his floral gift.

"Thank you. Since this is our first official outing, I thought a special dress was in order." She smelled the flowers. "They are beautiful, Fraser. You picked the right color."

"I have an army of spies who are determined to make sure I treat you well." He leaned close to her ear. "Mrs. Barton told me you were wearing lavender. Now, we had best be off. I want everyone to see you on my arm."

Her shawl in place and her nosegay in hand, she took his arm and got into the carriage.

"I spoke with Mr. Spivey's protégé today, Richard Younge." He heard her quick intake of breath above the noise of the carriage. "Is something amiss?"

"No, no, not at all." Here is her opportunity. Just a casual comment, *I'm planning a reception for Richard. He is a distant relative.*

But Fraser wouldn't leave it be. He'd ask questions, and she would defend her reasons. No, it wasn't how she wanted to spend the evening. After the theater, that's when she'd tell him.

"He called on me today. It seems he thinks he's going to win the election. You would think he was running unopposed."

"What did he want?" Richard wouldn't say anything to Fraser, would he?

"That is what I'm trying to find out. Did you know that Younge was Aunt Adelaide's estate steward?" His question wasn't probing, but she squirmed under his nonchalant interrogation.

"I believe he had the position for a few weeks."

Tell him before someone does.

"Actually, from the time Uncle John passed away until early August. Kaiah doesn't like him. Neither does the staff."

The carriage pulled up to the theater, and he handed her down. Her touch on his arm made him turn. She was determined to straighten out this disaster.

"About the election. About Richard Younge."

"Fraser."

They both turned to see Barrington walking toward them with the Duchess of Stonehill.

"Lady Anna." The duchess came up to her.

"Is Effie with you?" Anna searched the crowd looking for her friend.

"No. She begged off this evening. I'm sure she would have joined us if she knew you were here." The duchess eyed the handsome duke, then gave Anna a glare saying… *introduce me.*

"My lady, may I present the Duke of Willbury? He is the great-nephew of the late Duke and Duchess of Willbury. Your Grace, the Duchess of Stonehill. I believe you know her husband, Owen, the Duke of Stonehill."

"Your Grace, I was looking forward to meeting you. I am so sorry for your loss. The duchess and I were good friends. I miss her terribly." Anna was well aware that the two duchesses argued something fierce, but before they departed, they would be laughing as if nothing happened.

"Thank you for your kind thoughts. Aunt Adelaide was a wonderful woman." Lovingly, that's how he described his great aunt, not with what he said, but rather how he said it.

"Ah, Willbury. I see you've met my good wife." Stonehill gave his wife a warm smile.

"My dear, I know you've wanted to speak to His Grace, but his presence is required."

"What I must do for the Crown." She put up her hand. "And just as we were getting acquainted. You, my husband, you needn't try to disguise your intentions. I noticed you engaged with Judge Scofield. What other reason could there be but business for the crown?" The duchess faced the newly minted duke. "Your Grace, it was a pleasure meeting you."

"As it was mine. If you will excuse us." Anna and the duchess watched as the men navigated the crowded floor.

"I must congratulate you on your fine catch." The duchess was still watching him.

"I haven't reeled him in." If asked, Anna would admit she enjoyed watching him and the response of others. Further, if she had to put it into a word, she would say proud.

"You best not let anyone know, or you'll have half the women in this room parading their daughters, sisters, or nieces in front of him. And the other half will offer for him themselves."

The Duchess of Stonehill turned from looking after the men to Anna. "Don't look so surprised. All of London is talking about the new duke. He scares most girls, but you and my Effie could handle him."

Effie? Anna's stomach sank at the idea of someone else with Fraser, let alone her close friend. Would Effie and Fraser be a good match? Her penchant for ginger biscuits alone would endear her to him. The idea made her smile, but she was aware that both her friends were much deeper than that.

Effie was a gentle soul who was comfortable to be with. She wasn't judgmental, she listened, and she helped her friends talk out issues. She was fair-minded and trustworthy.

Anna blinked, not wanting to validate what in her heart of hearts was true. Effie would be perfect for him.

"There's Lady Wynnstan. You'll forgive me. I wanted to speak to her before the performance began."

"Of course. Go right ahead."

Without another word, the duchess hurried toward the punch bowl.

"I see Her Grace has abandoned you. I've come to your rescue." Fraser handed her a playbill. "We should take to our seats before the crush."

"What were you two conspiring to do?" He took her elbow as they climbed the grand staircase.

"Her Grace told me you are the talk of London." They nodded to a few people as they passed.

"You say that as if it is something to be desired." He leaned close to her. "It is not."

"She also said her Effie would be perfect for you." Anna worked at keeping her voice matter-of-fact.

"Oh? What is her given name?" His voice dropped to an intimate whisper.

"Euphemia. It's her great-grandmother's name."

"Eu-phe-mia." He drew out the syllables and made her name sound special.

She gave him a sideways glance. He couldn't do that with her name. Anna was short and sweet. Maybe Marianna. There was that devilish look in his eyes, as if he could read her mind. Really?

"She was one of the ladies that visited when we were playing whist."

"How convenient. You won't have to introduce us." He looked off into the distance. "I could pay her a visit at tea."

He caught a glimpse of her disappointment and immediately regretted his teasing.

"You know I am jesting."

"Please, don't apologize. By all means, call on Effie. There is a soiree at the circulating library at the end of the week. You can be her escort."

"That isn't necessary." *She didn't know I was jesting?*

They reached the top of the grand staircase and stepped to the side.

"Don't fight me about this. I understand why you weren't interested in the other women I recommended, but there is nothing negative you can say about Lady Euphemia Brandt. She is perfect for you."

They continued on toward their box. With each step, he regretted his foolish taunting.

"Do you have a beau, or someone you like?"

"How do you know that I haven't already got my sights on someone? And what makes you ask?"

"I'm interested in what attributes attract you in a man. How else can I find the right gentleman for you? Better than the one you pine for now. Or how much work I need to do to mend my ways, to be an example to the fortunate fellow."

Anna shook her head and chuckled. That's more like his Anna. He laughed along with her.

"If you don't tell me what attracts you to a man, you risk having me figure it out for myself, which can be dangerous."

Anna said nothing. They kept walking toward their seats.

"Then tell me what type of man attracts your friend Effie." They reached his box, and Anna faced him.

"Effie would like a man with integrity, compassion, and especially one who is not afraid of a woman with ability and a good mind. That should give you a lot to work on. You are fortunate she is not particular about a man being handsome."

"And you will, of course, test me on all my attributes, for your friend."

She smiled serenely but said nothing.

They stepped through the dark curtain and stood in the small space before the door. He reached around her for the latch, bringing him a step or two away.

She fought an overwhelming need to step even closer. His proximity was both intoxicating and dangerous. Their childhood teasing had definitely taken an adult turn which, by all that was holy, she enjoyed.

He moved closer, so close she saw nothing else but him. She didn't move. Was she too trusting, too honest? Brick by brick, her defenses crumbled. Anna held her breath.

Here they stood. Alone, inches apart, but all she could do was stare at his chest. She was afraid to see what was in his eyes. She took a breath and was filled with the scent of lavender and citrus. His scent.

He tipped her head back with a gentle touch. She should say something off-putting or humorous to stop him, but when she gazed into his eyes, she was caught like a moth drawn to a burning candle.

The mischievous look she saw moments ago was gone. Instead, his extraordinary eyes glowed with mystery, longing, and a spark of some indefinable emotion. How could one look reveal so much? He moved a fraction closer. Her eyes fluttered closed, and his mouth covered hers.

His kiss was gentle, merely a pressing together of their lips. She should… The thought escaped her.

He nibbled her lower lip ever so gently.

Dizzy and lightheaded, her heart hammered, but she didn't want him to stop. She gave herself willingly to the passion of his kiss. Boldly, she parted her lips, inviting him in.

He groaned softly, and she drew her arms around him, holding him close as he deepened his kiss.

He pulled away and gently brushed a stray strand of hair from her forehead.

"I would stay here rather than watch the play, but the others will be arriving, and we'll be in the way."

She licked her lips, enjoying the taste of him. He gave her a quick kiss on her nose, smiled, and took a full step back.

"Are you ready?"

Her hands skimmed down her skirt, and her heart settled into a steadier beat. Her cheeks had time to cool before they took their seats.

He stopped her hands from fussing by clasping them in his own.

The unexpected touch made her heart race. She lifted her head and gazed into his eyes.

"You look fine. Better than fine." His low, mellow voice soothed her nerves.

He reached behind her and unlatched the door. They stepped into the box. She took the seat closer to the rail and fanned herself with the playbill. Fraser sat behind her. Looking around, a frisson of fear swept through her.

Secrets? Or untruths?

Did it matter?

Fraser spoke to someone in the next box. She glanced over her shoulder to see who sat there, afraid it would be Richard.

Richard. She had to tell him, even though she declined to have the reception at Raven Hall. It would be a moot point, except she knew better than most people the value he put on truth and full disclosure. She had to tell him.

Moments later, the door behind them opened and their two friends joined them. Mrs. Bainbridge took the seat next to her, and Lord Barrington sat next to Fraser.

"It seems this box is the center of attention," Mrs. Bainbridge said.

Anna looked at the people sitting below and in the other boxes. Almost all eyes were on them.

"It must be Willbury. Everyone wants to see the new duke. What other reason could there be?" Anna busied herself reading the playbill.

"His Grace has done well in his campaign." Mrs. Bainbridge chuckled.

Anna turned in her seat and faced her friend. "Campaign?"

"Mr. Hawkins has been very busy." She took the Sommer Sentinel out of her reticule and handed it to her.

Anna read the article then dropped it into her lap.

"This has Willbury and I all but married." She looked around the theater and understood. "That is why everyone is staring at us."

She turned in her seat and handed Willbury the Sentinel.

He leaned forward. "I read the article earlier."

"And you didn't say anything to me?"

"This is exactly what we wanted people to believe. I would say you and I have been most successful. We are a very accomplished team."

A chime sounded. "The performance is beginning. Perhaps I should give you a tender kiss for all to see."

Horrified. She turned around as he softly chuckled.

They didn't speak during the performance, nor at intermission. Their box was filled with well-wishers. All she could do was smile.

Thankfully, right before the curtain came down, they withdrew from the theater. She and Fraser sat facing each other in his carriage on their way to The Willow for a light supper. Barrington and Mrs. Bainbridge followed in Barrington's carriage.

"You must know that I would never do anything to compromise you. You usually take my teasing in stride, but I may have taken it too far tonight. I am truly sorry if I offended you."

Did he regret kissing her? She turned away from him, afraid he would see her disappointment.

"Not kissing you in the dark, never that, but to tease that I would kiss you in public."

"That is a relief." She kept looking out the carriage window. "This game we are playing. There are times I am not sure what is make-believe and what is real."

He leaned across the small space that separated them and took her hands. She turned and gazed at him. "There are things I tease you about, but know this: I do not give my kisses lightly to anyone. I hold them sacred."

He held her stare a bit longer, then released her hands, and sat back where he was lost in the darkness.

"I appreciate your position. I do not play games with my kisses either. I hold them as a precious declaration."

"As do I." His voice another shadow in the carriage.

She dared to glance at him from under her lashes and came to a realization. Fraser was courting her. Plain and simple.

Her heart soared.

Chapter Fourteen

They sat in the conservatory amongst the fragrant flowers and dined service à la française. Decanters of wine, the cold meats, cheeses, savory pastry creations, and confections, with the obligatory apple tarts and ginger biscuits, were set on the table for them to serve themselves. At this late hour, he had dismissed most of the staff.

"I enjoyed the performance." Anna ate a ginger biscuit. The evening was perfect. Their game was complete. Both of them were winners.

"As did I." Willbury sat next to her and poured the last of the wine into her glass while Barrington and Mrs. Bainbridge strolled through the conservatory.

"If you will excuse me. I need to replenish our supply." He held up the empty decanter.

"I'll go with you. I don't think Barrington or Mrs. Bainbridge will miss us."

He helped her up, tucked her arm into his, and led the way to the drawing room. He opened the sideboard and looked through the various bottles while she continued her inspection.

Barrington and Mrs. Bainbridge entered. Mrs. Bainbridge joined Anna on the settee while Barrington helped Willbury.

"Just in time for some Madeira." Willbury poured four glasses.

"Honoria!" Barrington grabbed the back of the nearby chair, his face a mask of pain.

Mrs. Bainbridge turned, hearing the distress in Barrington's voice. Her expression changed from puzzled to concerned. She jumped to her feet, and she hurried to his side.

Willbury assisted Barrington to the chaise. The wine was forgotten.

Barrington's war injury had everyone, including his medical team, certain he would never walk again. He worked hard to recover and proved them all wrong. The injury did have lingering effects even after all these years.

"Would you mind if we made an early night of it? There are times when my body can forecast the weather better than any witch in the area. Right now, it's predicting rain and a lot of it."

"Not at all. Rest while I have your carriage brought around."

Mrs. Bainbridge gathered her things as well as Barrington's and pulled Anna aside.

"You haven't told Willbury of your involvement with Richard." Mrs. Bainbridge's disapproving glare made her uncomfortable.

"No. I have tried." She squirmed like a new student being reprimanded at the seminary.

"Not hard enough. You know gossip runs rampant. With everyone talking about you and Willbury, anything that would put that union in jeopardy will be the major topic of discussion and almost impossible to overcome. You have seen how this game is played.

"It would be best if he heard what he needs to know from you and not from anyone else. I taught you better than that."

Anna stood glued to the spot saying nothing. Being scolded was bad enough, but disappointing the headmistress was worse. Her friend was correct. She looked on as Willbury helped Barrington.

"Half a truth is often a great lie. Mr. Franklin was not wrong. You know Willbury well enough. Truth, the whole truth, is a value he will not compromise."

Mrs. Bainbridge helped Barrington on with his coat and, together with Willbury and Anna, went to the foyer.

Mr. Barton appeared at the door. "Let me, Your Grace."

Barrington put his arm around the butler's shoulder, and they walked to the carriage.

"Thank you. It was a lovely evening." Mrs. Bainbridge stood close by as Barrington's driver and Mr. Barton helped him into the landau, then handed her into the carriage.

Willbury closed the door and stood by the window.

"It was indeed a good evening. Reese, I'll call on you tomorrow." He nodded at Mrs. Bainbridge. "Send someone if you need me."

He stood back, and with a wave, the carriage was off. Anna stood next to him as they watched the carriage make its way to the road.

"We could both use a whiskey after that." Willbury took Anna's hand, and they walked back into the drawing room.

"Would you prefer a whiskey or port?" He stood with his back to her. "Whiskey, I think. There's no need to be nervous or overly concerned about Barrington. He's in good hands."

She hadn't given thought to Barrington, at least not at this moment. She kept hearing *half-truth* echo in her head. How did she allow this situation to get so out of hand?

He handed her a glass of the tawny liquid. Moments ago, she craved to be with him. Now, all she wanted to do was run in the opposite direction. He would never forgive her. She drank the whiskey, put down the glass, and gathered her wrap. The evening was too perfect. She didn't want to do anything to spoil it. *Coward.* Since when was she afraid to take responsibility for her actions? Tell him and get it over with.

"It's best I return home."

His stare made her as uncomfortable as her corset and had the same effect. Her breathing was constricted and shallow. Escape was her only alternative. She headed for the door, intent on leaving.

"Wait. I'll take you to Raven Hall." He gulped the last of his whiskey and hurried to catch up to her.

"That won't be necessary. The walk will do me good." She fussed with the door.

He covered her hand with his.

"Anna. What's wrong? I've never seen you like this. I assure you. Barrington will be fine. You'll not walk home alone."

She took a calming breath.

He opened the door and led her toward the stable where he quickly had his gig ready.

"Is it the attention we received at the theater?" he asked, handing her up to the carriage. "I should have warned you, told you what would likely happen."

He was making it worse. Yes, she knew what to expect, but by all that was holy, she also had it in her mind how he would react to her involvement with Richard's campaign.

She studied him as he maneuvered the vehicle onto the road. Once he knew the entire story, they would never be this close again.

She could see the next item in the Sommer Sentinel.

A duke returns to the marriage market. Lady A returns to the shelf.

Chapter Fifteen

"I understand that your cousin Richard is hoping to be the representative of our borough." They slowly proceeded down the road.

A small wave of panic ran up her spine. Truth. Nothing else. She swallowed hard. Stick to the facts and truth. There was no reason why she shouldn't help Richard.

"He wanted my help." There. That wasn't as difficult as she thought. However, it was with great difficulty that she kept her voice even and her tone matter-of-fact. Anna kept her focus on the road ahead. She was well aware one glance at him and her carefully constructed façade would crumble.

"How are you helping him? No disrespect, but campaigns are handled by a candidate's campaign manager."

"I am helping him but only with a reception. Certainly not his campaign." And why shouldn't she help him with his campaign?

"You're planning his reception? No one else?" He glared at her with a lethal calmness.

Didn't he know that people sought her out to orchestrate their events? The Duchess of Northumberland had asked for her assistance more than once.

"Yes. I've hosted events, soirees, meetings, and balls with great success. This one will be no different."

His eyes darkened more if that were possible. They continued along. Raven Hall wasn't much farther.

"Fraser. What is wrong? We both know Richard."

"I didn't realize you were so close to him. I remember him as an awfully mean-spirited fellow."

She should have asked Barrington for a ride back to Raven Hall. What she truly regretted was not having this discussion with Fraser sooner. Both Mrs. Bainbridge and Mrs. Cutler had advised her.

"Have you seen him often?"

She turned away without replying. What should she tell him? How would she tell him? *He's visited two or three times a week since early August.* No. No. That will never do.

"Should I take that as a 'yes'?"

Anna felt the shock run across her usually constrained face. "I didn't say that."

They turned onto the Raven Hall drive and came to a stop at the door.

He handed her down. She hurried into the house, surprised he followed behind her.

"There are questions about your cousin and his sponsor, Spivey." They stood in the drawing room.

A shiver of apprehension rushed down her spine at the mention of the sponsor's name. She poured him a brandy and one for herself, managing to keep her hand steady.

"You are too trusting and innocent in the ways of politics." She heard the irritation in his tone and the thread of warning in his voice.

Her emotions ran rampant. One minute she was apprehensive, and the next she was annoyed. He was treating her as an errant child, and her patience was wearing thin.

"I appreciate your concern for my well-being, but I will be the judge of what I am capable or not capable of doing."

"Politics is not a parlor game. It's dangerous and cunning—"

"I am well aware there are two different types of people in this world. Those that are honest and trustworthy, and those that are not." Why was she arguing with him? She agreed with him.

Richard was not worth losing him. *Losing him?* She spun around and faced him. She had never seen him so angry.

"I did not offer to coordinate Richard's reception—"

"Running a campaign is costly, and Richard Younge hasn't the blunt to fund his campaign. His own father does not support his running."

"I'm told he doesn't need his father's support. He has Mr. Spivey."

"Another questionable character."

"On that we both agree. Last month I received a letter—"

"You must distance yourself from Richard and his campaign at once." He finished his drink in one gulp and poured another.

Her glass was halfway to her mouth when she stopped.

"I see you are upset."

"I'm more than upset." He put the untouched glass down. "I thought you had better judgment, better standards. Really, Anna. Richard?"

"This reception was to be a simple event. He told me his election was secure, that he had no opposition." She had gotten this far. Now was the time to tell him everything and end this useless battle.

"You must cut all ties with him at once."

He wasn't listening to a single word she said. Not about the letter or how Richard had lied about being unopposed.

She would not be intimidated by him.

"Mrs. Cutler can send your regrets."

Nor would she let him tell her what to do or how to do it. Anna swallowed hard not to reveal her building anger, but she was never good at keeping what she thought behind her teeth, and he had gone too far.

"I regret to inform Your Grace that I am not one of your subordinates. You cannot order me to do anything. Thank you for an enjoyable evening. You know the way out."

He stepped closer to her. His eyes, his beautiful blue-green eyes were dark with anger. The slash of his mouth, the one that kissed her so tenderly and fully hours ago was an ugly grimace.

"I hope you both are very happy."

He turned toward the door, then hesitated. "At least one of us found our mate. I thought, for a brief moment, we had found each other. I see now that our courtship was exactly as we planned, a ploy. No, *you* played it as a game. Congratulations."

Mate? Courtship? What was he talking about? Before she could move or say anything, he stormed out of the room. The front door slammed with a note of finality.

She ran and pulled open the door as the gig raced toward the road at a breakneck speed. It careened on one wheel as he took the turn too fast. She held her breath ready to run toward him, but the gig righted itself and sped away taking him down the road and, she feared, out of her life.

Anna returned to the drawing room in a daze. How did this wonderful, lovely night turn into this?

"I came as quickly as I could." Mrs. Cutler hurried in. "Was that His Grace who stormed out in such a huff?"

Anna stood in the center of the room, her chin quivering, trying to hold back her tears. Mrs. Cutler took her in her arms and drew her to the settee.

"He ordered me to withdraw my help from Richard and his sponsor. He commanded me. He thinks I want Richard. *Richard!* Where did he get that idea?" Tears rolled down her cheeks. She stared out the window.

"I love him. I've always loved him. Now, I'll never see him again."

"All is not lost. This is a misunderstanding. It can be resolved."

"Do you expect him to forgive me?"

Mrs. Cutler straightened and looked at her with wise eyes. "The question is will you forgive him for being narrow-minded and a bully. As well as being jealous."

Anna stared at the housekeeper blankly.

"Why else would he be so upset?"

Anna's fingertips lightly touched her lips. She closed her eyes, and for a moment, a brief moment, she could feel his firm, sensual lips and a tinge of the dizzying journey on which he took her.

"His Grace kindly told me politics is a man's game. He's the same as every other man I know." She closed her eyes. "I want to cry. Not only for losing him but losing who I thought he was."

The brass knocker struck the door and echoed through the hall.

Her heart leapt to her throat. He came back. Anna hurried down the hall. She would make him understand, promise…

Elated and hopeful, Anna pulled open the door and stared in confusion.

Richard stood slouched against the door jam, half into his cups.

All hope dashed, she held on to the door, dazed as her confusion turned from disappointment to despair.

He straightened to his full height. Slowly and seductively, his gaze slid down her body.

"Where have you been?" He held up his hand to stop her from answering and swayed unsteady on his feet. He leaned close to her.

She turned her head away from the stench of the cheap whiskey on his breath.

"I know where you were and who you were with."

Anna said nothing as he pushed past her on unsteady legs and went into the drawing room.

"Everyone knows." He turned around, stumbling in place. "It's all over the village. Even in the London paper."

He fumbled in his pocket and pulled the offending paper out, shaking it in her face.

"Everyone is laughing at you. Oh, the men are slapping Willbury on his back. Job well done, they're saying. Don't say I didn't warn you about him. He is not what you think he is, and I can show you." He took her arm. "Come, we'll go now, and I'll show you who the Duke of Willbury really is."

"Sit down and we can talk about it." She removed Richard's hand from her arm.

He shoved her hand away.

"You are all that is important to me. You would make the perfect wife for a politician. And I am ready to marry and have a family. You have no prospects, and you told me you have no plans to embarrass yourself with a third defeat in the London Season."

"Richard, it's late and time for you to leave. I can have one of the footmen see you…"

"No. I see what you are doing." He grabbed her by her shoulders. "You'll marry me and be glad of it. You belong to me. Me. No one else. I saw the way Willbury stormed out of here. He doesn't want you. You should be grateful that I do."

Richard turned at a movement from the doorway. Mr. Cutler and two footmen stepped into the room.

He released her shoulders and straightened his coat.

"You're right." He moved away from her. "It is late. We can talk about our plans tomorrow when I return from Newcastle. But you will never see Willbury again. Never."

He headed out of the room and the house.

Mr. Cutler nodded to the footmen.

"Where are they going?" The men looked at Mr. Cutler then at Anna.

"They're going to make certain that Mr. Younge gets home."

Chapter Sixteen

"My lady, I've returned from Lord Haworth." The footman stood at the door to the carriage. It was morning, and she and Mrs. Cutler were on their way to The Willow.

She held out her hand for the message from her father.

"Oh no, my lady. Your father was on his way out and didn't have time to write a response. I am to tell you. *Richard.* That's all he said. Is there a reply?"

"No. Nothing. Thank you." The man nodded and motioned to the driver.

The carriage proceeded down the smooth drive.

"I asked my father the cause of the disagreement between him and Francis Younge."

"Richard. Why am I not surprised?" Mrs. Cutler shook her head. "He's not to be trusted."

"It is more than Richard and his games at this point."

"You don't have to go to The Willow." Mrs. Cutler sat across the carriage from Anna.

"Yes, I do. I gave my word."

They went the rest of the way in silence. The carriage arrived at The Willow. Mrs. Barton met them and led them to the library.

"There are some repairs being made to the drawing room before this Sunday's reception. His Grace has given us access to his library since he is expected to be out the rest of the day."

She wandered around admiring the objects de art and the books. "As many times as I've been here, I don't remember being in this room."

"This was the previous duke's room. Her Grace all but closed off the library after he passed on. She found it difficult to be in here with so much of him still present. I think our new duke prefers to be in here rather than the other more formal rooms."

"It does feel personal." Anna continued around the room until she came to the fireplace. She gazed at the portrait of the Duke and Duchess of Willbury that hung over the mantel.

"My lady. Cook made cider for you to sample." Mrs. Barton handed her a glass filled with the amber liquid.

She sipped and closed her eyes. "Just as I remember. My thanks to Cook."

Anna was drawn once again to the portrait.

"It is a beautiful picture of the duke and duchess. She was no more than twenty, and he a stately twenty-eight," Mrs. Barton said as she organized the papers for one final review.

"They're both very handsome, dressed for court." Anna stared at the picture, imagining Duchess's quick wit and…

The cider dripped over the edge of her glass, splashing down the front of her pelisse.

"Lady Anna?" Mrs. Cutler removed the glass from her hand and noticed she was still staring at the picture.

"I'm so sorry." Recovered from her momentary shock, she looked down and stared at the stain. "I was admiring the picture, and the glass slipped from my hand."

"This was their favorite portrait. I think that's one of the reasons Her Grace didn't use this room. It's the only picture with a likeness of her husband. It's a portrait of their wedding day."

Anna hadn't taken her eyes off the delicate folds of the bodice, and the gem pinned to the sash at the duchess's waist.

"Her Grace would be devastated if she knew the gem has been misplaced." Anna stared at Mrs. Cutler. Her housekeeper took a step closer to her.

"Could she have sold it?" Anna asked the question but knew the answer. The duchess's gem was on her desk at Raven Hall.

"No." Mrs. Barton went on. "She would never sell that piece. The brooch is part of the family history. The initials AR are engraved on the back."

"Adelaide Reinsford."

"Not at all. The gem is a betrothal gift passed down by each duke to his duchess. The tradition started in the 8th century when the first Duke of Willbury asked for the hand of Princess Aline Roumieu. The initials are hers. Since then, it has been in the keeping of every duchess, a gift from her duke. Her Grace would never part with it willingly. She kept it close. After her husband's death, she pinned it to her nightrail every evening. I see your glass is empty. I'll be right back with some more."

"The brooch Her Grace is wearing." She nodded toward the portrait.

Mrs. Cutler tilted her head as she examined the piece.

Anna observed her as the woman's eyes widened. The housekeeper faced her. "It's the one Mr. Younge gave you."

Anna leaned close to her. "Yes, it is." Her voice was a whisper. "I fear everything Willbury cautioned me about Richard may be true."

"You must return the piece to him and explain what happened."

"No, not until I know a way to stop Richard. Willbury thinks I'm not capable. I must prove to him that I am."

"You can't go around trying to convince men that women are capable. That is a losing battle."

"I agree. But I can prove to this man that this woman"—she tapped her chest—"that I am competent."

"How? What do you plan to do?"

"I'm not sure, but we can work on that when we're back at Raven Hall. I need to think of a way to resolve the issue with Willbury first."

"Here we are." Mrs. Barton set a platter on the table. "I brought some ginger biscuits as well."

"Come in, Willbury." Barrington stood by the sideboard gathering papers. "Have a seat at the table. Scofield and I were just going to look at the documents."

Barrington made his way to the library table with barely a limp.

"Should you be walking about?" Willbury glanced at the judge, who shrugged and shook his head. He should know better. Barrington couldn't be kept down.

"I am perfectly fine. You came at the right time. I received these documents on the Saxton case from Edward."

"I'm interested why you opened this inquiry. This case is nearly ten years old. Besides, I thought you retired." Scofield was the type of judge that wanted justice, no matter how long it took.

"Retired? Not at all. Simply a pause until I get estate issues settled, then move back to London. This is a special interest case. It appears that some of the stolen items Saxton was accused of taking may never have been in his possession. The items were never removed from the premises. Whoever filed the report had it all wrong."

"I didn't want to see Lloyd Saxton sent to New South Wales, but I find what you're saying impossible to believe." Scofield searched through the folio, pulled out a document, and handed it to Willbury. "This is the list of stolen items."

He read through the list, nodding his agreement. "Yes, this is the court document." He turned the page, then searched the folio. "I don't see the affidavit that attests this is accurate. There's no signature on this."

"He wasn't found guilty because of the trinkets. It was the money. All along, Saxton claimed it was Younge. Their relationship made it difficult. Lloyd Saxton was the steward. Richard Younge worked for Lloyd. There is speculation Richard registered the complaint. It was the incriminating evidence found in Saxton's kit that decided the case. There was no other alternative but to find him guilty."

"Don't you think that's odd? That he would hold on to incriminating evidence? He could have tossed it out a window or dropped it on the floor rather than put it into his kit. No. Something is not right. That's what made me look through the documents."

"Even if you find that Saxton didn't commit the crime, he cannot get back the years he spent in New South Wales."

"No, but he could clear his and his family's name. It would be good for his brother."

"I hope you succeed." The judge stood ready to leave. "I don't like to see innocent people suffering, but I think you have very little evidence to go on." Scofield gathered his papers. "I must be off but keep me informed. I will do all I can for you. Gentlemen."

Barrington nodded as the judge left and smiled. Several moments later, Mrs. Bainbridge walked through the door.

"I just saw the judge on his way out. He told me to make sure you rest. You're walking around too much."

Barrington chuckled at the judge's concern. "He is from the old school. If I sat, the muscles would seize up even worse. No, the hot compresses and exercise have eased the stiffness."

"I brought you a book from the library to keep you busy while you sit and recuperate. And don't call me old school. You can read while the hot compresses do their job."

"Aye, aye, admiral." He gave her a mock salute.

She turned to Willbury. "And for you, Your Grace, I've brought the recent edition of the Sommer Sentinel."

"You have my thanks." He took the folded paper and put it to the side.

"Not interested. I think this item will draw your attention."

Mrs. Bainbridge picked up the paper and turned to a specific page.

Lady A is in such demand that another has tried to usurp her duke's position. Lady A is flattered by the offer, but she graciously declined. Assuredly, dear reader, a duke holds her heart.

She placed the paper on the table in front of him, folded in such a fashion he couldn't help but see the article.

"What has happened that Lady A is compelled to use the Sommer Sentinel as a means of communicating with you?"

"I admit I didn't handle things well last night. Younge told me his fiancée was planning his reception."

"I see. And she told you she was planning his reception, and of course, you gave her no opportunity to explain?"

Willbury bitterly regretted the way the evening ended. He found it impossible to sleep. Pangs of guilt kept him awake.

"She is naive and has no idea about politics and how that game is played." His explanation rang false even to him.

He read Anna's message in the paper. His heartbeat stumbled, hesitated, the next beats growing faster until it was like being in the Old Bailey, standing in front of the judge seconds before he gives his verdict.

"First you have to decide if you want her."

"I do." He answered without giving a second thought.

"Why don't you and Reese plan to call at the seminary later today? One o'clock or so would be good. You may find me entertaining Anna."

"Honoria. Are you conspiring?"

She looked at Barrington under her brow, smiled, and said nothing.

Barrington picked up her hand and kissed it. "I am glad you are on my side."

Chapter Seventeen

Wrapped in her wool shawl, Anna stood at her bedroom window focused on the dark silhouettes in the garden as they brightened and took shape with the lightening day. In the distance, she saw the occasional white caps with the rising and falling of the sea. The movement was rhythmic, almost hypnotic.

Sleep had escaped her last night as she tossed and turned, unable to quiet her mind. Finally, she abandoned her bed and sat at the small writing table scribbling her thoughts.

Richard had taken Lady Adelaide's gem. What else did he have? He wouldn't be satisfied with only the gem. Calling him out would prove nothing. He wouldn't tell her the truth. One item he might be able to lie his way out. He did when Mrs. Cutler caught him with the empty tart tray. However, if she found other things he had taken and confronted him with them all she might be successful.

She had thought it out and saw no other way. Her plan was simple. Search Richard's house. He lived in a modest area filled with small homes. A place where shop owners and workers lived. He had gone to Newcastle this morning, and Mrs. Cutler would be at the market. With no one to interfere, it was an excellent opportunity for her to take action and test her plan.

To remain unnoticed, she dressed in the morning clothes she wore to the duchess's funeral. No one took notice of a grieving woman and with the black veil covering her face; no one would know who she was.

She dressed quickly, stood in front of the mirror, and put her veil in place. Satisfied no one would recognize her, she left the house for her trek across the field.

An hour later and worn out from her hike, she was at the edge of the village almost at the road to Harrogate. Her clothes were covered with road dust, but her determination didn't waver. She dusted herself off as best she could, then walked into the small square as if she belonged there.

As it was market day, several stalls filled the area. The aroma of fresh baked bread drew people to the baker's table where a small line formed. Children ran after each other in a game of distract and grab, targeting the fruit vendor who swatted at them. People hurried along to their destination acknowledging one another, even her.

She walked down the rutted street bustling with carts and a steady flow of people in the direction of Richard's address. Anna peered between the buildings until she saw his house. She turned down his street and encountered fewer people as she walked down the lane. By the time she passed his house, there was no one else in sight.

The cottage itself was nothing remarkable, close to the road, low leggy shrubs filled the small front garden. As she passed, she noticed a sizable bleak back garden enclosed by a vine-covered wall.

She didn't want to bring attention to herself and, to that end, hesitated to go to the front door. She took notice that the windows were dark, and she saw no activity inside.

She turned down the lane that went behind the cottage and navigated the mud and muck as she searched for an opening. Somewhere in the middle of the wall, a small door stood ajar. She cautiously stepped through the opening, her footfalls quiet from sinking into soft mud as she fought her way through overgrown grass and vines.

By all that was holy, she stood looking at the back of the cottage. Her heart was beating a fast tattoo. She had no idea what she would do if someone confronted her.

Move. You can't just stand here like a statue. You've come this far. There is no turning back now.

Her shoulders back and her chin held high, she went up to the back door as if it was something she did every day and tried the latch. It was locked.

There was no avoiding trying the front door. Her heart thumped loudly as she followed the slope of the land along the back of the house. Hidden by a bush, she found a small path that led to the cellar. More willing to attempt entering this way, she hurried to the door.

With renewed determination, she pulled the latch hard. It opened. Excitement and fear jumbled together. She peered inside the dark cellar and waited for her eyes to adjust. As the room came into view, she swallowed hard and entered.

The area was filled with a jumble of crates and barrels in no particular order. She couldn't look in each one.

Plan. Stay with your plan.

She stepped forward and saw the staircase to the floor above on the far side of the room. Maneuvering around the obstacles, she climbed the steps. With her ear to the door, she listened for any sound that would tell her to abandon her mission. But all she heard was the thumping of her own heart.

Concentrate. Do what needs to be done and then be gone.

There were no footsteps or soft voices, no clocks ticking or aroma of food cooking. Certain that no one was home, she opened the door. A crack at first. Finally, she opened enough to slide through. The plan of the cottage was simple, two rooms on this floor and a ladder leading up to the attic loft. She decided to search the far room first.

The room was utilitarian. Nothing fancy. A bed, a cupboard, and a table next to the bed. No pictures or knickknacks strewn about or even a carpet on the floor. She went through the cupboard, checked under the mattress, and found nothing.

On the bedside table, she found a letter in a woman's hand. She quickly read it. *By all that is holy.* With care, she replaced the note as she found it.

She investigated the main room, examined the furniture, rummaged through every drawer, searched under the carpet, behind the items on the shelves, and even looked for a loose stone in the hearth. In the small writing desk, she found paper, ink, and a quill. A quick scan of the document, and her heart nearly came out of her chest.

Activity on the street increased. She put the paper back in the desk. Afraid she didn't have much more time, she looked at the attic steps and noticed the trail of dust from her skirts. Panicking, she tore the bottom of her petticoat and cleaned where she'd been.

Voices on the path to the front door reached her ears. She quickly went through the cellar door, closing it behind her as the front door opened.

Standing at the top of the steps, she listened to hear what was happening. Footsteps crossed the room and disappeared into the bedroom.

Anna carefully went down the stairs. Her only thought was to get out. As she hurried across the cellar, she noticed a large velvet pouch with the Willbury crest tucked under a shelf.

She removed the pouch, untied the rope, and opened it. Inside, she saw the cream jug and sugar bowl that matched the duchess's teapot.

Lord Reese, Scofield, and possibly Willbury must see this, but she couldn't remove anything. Richard would simply say she took it from the house. There had to be a way for her to bring them here. Her thoughts were interrupted by footsteps directly over her head.

She closed the bag, intending to return it to its spot but couldn't put the bag where she found it. The footsteps retreated. Maneuvering to replace the bag, she reached behind and pulled out the late duke's sword. She tucked the sword and pouch back where she found it. As she got to her feet, several crates burnished with the Willbury crest came into view. She cast an eye over the cellar and understood what she needed to do to incriminate Richard.

Anna hurried and reached out for the latch to the outside when the door to the first floor opened. Light spilled into the cellar. She pulled down her veil, shoved her hands into her pockets, and flattened against a hollow in the wall behind the storage shelves. It wasn't until the person started coming down the stairs that she saw the filthy piece of linen from her petticoat lying near the velvet bag.

He came down three steps and leaned over the railing. She strained, peering between the storage shelves and held her breath. It was Richard. He pulled a bottle of wine from the top of the crate, returned upstairs, and closed the door.

Breathing hard, she remained frozen against the wall for several long moments. What would have happened if he found her? There was too much at stake for him to simply let her go. Now she knew how foolish this adventure was. She would admonish herself later. Right now, she had to get out.

She grabbed the dirty rag, made her way to the door, and went out. She saw no one, and the back fence would provide cover as long as she stayed in the shadows. Anna went along the fence looking for the way out. Poking her hand between the vines, she moved down the fence but found nothing. There was little she could do but venture out into the sunlit portion of the wall. Before she took another step, someone grabbed her and pulled her through to the other side.

A hand was clamped over her mouth. "Not a word," was whispered in her ear. Anna turned. She couldn't believe her eyes.

"Mrs. Cutler?"

She put her index finger against her lips.

Anna nodded and quietly followed her housekeeper to a gig that stood close by.

"You shouldn't have come here by yourself. Especially if you planned to rummage through his things. What if he walked in on you?"

"Willbury taught me how to defend myself when we were younger. Once you learn you never forget." She added that in for good measure.

"Even he told you not to depend on your 'skills.' This wasn't a childhood prank. If he had caught you, being a Ravencroft wouldn't have saved you."

"I went inside to see what I could find." She dusted off her skirt and turned to her friend. "And what are you doing here?"

"Trying to keep you out of trouble. I saw you cross the field wearing that black dress and knew you were up to something. I never thought it would be this. I had no time to call anyone, so I came by myself." She took a breath.

"This excursion was an education. Aside from finding out I do not ever want to do this again, I found bottles of the late duke's wine. Larceny carries a harsh punishment. I needed to be sure before I said anything. Bottles of wine might be a gift, even a crate or two, but not fine silver, the duke's sword, or rare jewelry. And there may be more. I need to look through my father's documents before I say anything."

They rode in silence as Mrs. Cutler made a quick trip of it. Anna's mission had been successful. Willbury needed this information more, if that was even possible, than reconciling with her. As soon as they reached Raven Hall, Anna hurried into the library and searched through her father's papers. She methodically went through one drawer after another.

"What are we trying to find?"

Anna looked up from the desk at Mrs. Cutler amid a stack of papers. "A letter from Francis. The one he sent when he moved up by the Tweed River." She paged through a stack of papers. "Wait, here it is."

She pulled the letter from the papers and placed it on the desk, then took a letter from her folio, the one from Francis Younge asking her to help Richard. She put them side by side.

She sat back in the chair as Mrs. Cutler scrutinized the two documents, then stood up, startled at what she saw.

"These letters were not written by the same person."

"You're correct. The letter Richard gave me requesting my help was not from his father at all. I recognized the handwriting when I saw some pages in his writing desk. It was the draft of this letter. There's more." Anna put the documents away. "I read a letter addressed to Richard. It was from his wife."

"His… Why does that not surprise me? What are you going to do?"

"Come with me while I change. I'm visiting Mrs. Bainbridge today. I'll speak to her and see what advice she may have."

Anna sat with Mrs. Bainbridge in the seminary drawing room. They had gone through the usual news of the day. Anna waited for a lull in their conversation before she began.

"I wanted to talk to you about a situation." Mrs. Bainbridge gazed at her, waiting for her to continue.

"It recently came to light that the letter I received from my cousin Francis requesting I help Richard was not penned by him."

Mrs. Bainbridge put down her teacup and squarely looked at Anna.

"Ladies."

They both turned toward the door. Lord Reese and Willbury walked in.

"Reese, just the person I wanted to see." Mrs. Bainbridge swept to his side. "I need your expertise in the library." She turned to Anna and Willbury. "Forgive me. We won't be long."

Anna almost laughed. The headmistress nearly dragged the poor man from the room.

Willbury handed Anna the Sommer Sentinel, folded to the article he wanted her to read, and took a seat facing her.

A duke is humbled by Lady A's most public declaration.

"I think that's the best course of action. Anything less would have had our names dragged through the mud for weeks." The last thing she wanted was to discuss last night, but one glance at Willbury registered his disappointment. Had he dared to think she would be placated so easily?

"How are your plans for tomorrow's library soiree proceeding? I'm looking forward to seeing your friend, Lady Euphemia." He met her eyes without flinching.

She was relieved he didn't want to pursue last night's argument and surprised he remembered Effie.

"It is all in good order. The last bit of managing takes place right before the event. Chaos happens during it.

"Regarding Effie. I'm sure you and she are well suited to each other. However, I do have a concern."

He gestured for her to continue.

"Effie is my dearest friend. She, too, has a mind of her own and is independent. She will not be relegated to the side and insists on being in the thick of things."

"Like you?"

He took her hand. "If I offended you, I am sorry. I spoke in haste out of fear you might put yourself in danger. While you are a very capable woman, with many talents, I have been in the political sphere and see what it can do to the strongest of people, men and women.

"As for Richard Younge. If he is the man you want."

"You needn't give Richard another thought. He may think he is marrying me, but that is one thing I can assure you will never happen." She put her hand over his. "Family is very important to me. He claimed that my support would help mend a long-time breach. That was the reason I agreed to help with his reception. I do understand and appreciate your concern."

But that didn't mean she would retreat from proving to him, or more importantly to herself, she was more than a woman who planned events.

"You will have to find me someone else, Your Grace." She gave him an aloof nod that eased the tension and brought a smile to his face.

Chapter Eighteen

The theme of the Miller Circulating Library event was *In Honor of the Printed Page*. Mrs. Miller thought the idea and the planned execution was clever. Everything was black and white. For many, this event, and the Harvest Ball later in the month, were the last events in Sommer-by-the-Sea before those who were attending the Season departed for London.

Anna had spent the afternoon decorating and preparing the rooms for the onslaught of people. Guests had been arriving for the last hour. After making certain the buffet and beverages were all arranged properly, Anna made her way to the front of the library where Mr. and Mrs. Miller greeted their guests. Mr. Miller wore an evening coat, and Mrs. Miller wore a white silk gown with a black cape.

She passed small groups of people congregating near the buffet and beverage tables. Some sat in the cozy reading areas scattered around the room. Many stood in small clusters chatting.

Everyone looked wonderful. Most of the men wore their dinner coats, and the women had Madam Pembroke, the modiste, up all hours for the last few weeks finishing their gowns for the evening. Many wore black, and some wore blue so dark one would think it was black.

Scofield and Lord Reese created a cordon around Willbury, protecting him from mothers who looked hungrily at an almost eligible, handsome, and wealthy duke. She, on the other hand, sailed through their blockade.

Willbury relieved a passing footman of a glass of cider, stepped closer to her, claiming his territory, and handed her the beverage.

"You look parched. You've been flittering around all evening."

She graciously took the cider, tempted to fortify it with some brandy, but thought better of it. With everything under control, she drank her cider and enjoyed their company.

"What else did you find out about the Saxton case?" Scofield asked Willbury.

"The two pouches of coins were taken from my great-uncle's library. Saxton was quickly identified because one pouch with several coins was found in his kit. Numerous witnesses attested that he was in the main house or the stable the entire time. It bothers me that the second pouch and the rest of the coins were never found. Based on the last time anyone saw the pouches and when they were reported missing, there was no time to do away with them."

Willbury eyed her with an apologetic smile.

"Without any other suspect and part of the stolen property found in his kit, the outcome was inevitable. We can discuss this another time. Let's not bore Lady Anna with this unpleasantness."

Anna wondered if the judge's opinion about the delicacy of women and their inability to deal with politics and law were similar to Willbury's.

She sipped her cider to stop from speaking. She would have told Willbury that the Saxton case was only one issue that implicated Richard. Adding forgery to his list of offenses, she wondered what else he was involved in.

"I hope you gentlemen are enjoying the soiree." Anna turned to Willbury. "I see you have a solid wall around you to deflect any intruders."

He chuckled and gave her a devastating smile.

"Actually, if you turn and look, you will see that your presence has done more to deter the intruders than the judge or Barrington ever could."

Her smile drooped as she noticed mothers simmering at their lost opportunity.

"Shall we take a turn around the room? A man courting a beautiful woman wants everyone to see his good fortune." He gave her his arm.

He still played the game. So be it. She would enjoy it while it lasted. She put down her empty glass and laced her arm through his.

They meandered through the crowd, stopped for Anna to graciously accept accolades for the party, and for people to acknowledge Willbury.

"I think we are a great success." Willbury nodded to Hawkins. "I haven't heard one mother tell me their daughter's attributes."

"Lady Anna." They stopped as Effie approached them. "This event gets better every year. Your Grace, it is good to see you again."

"Likewise, and please, Willbury will do."

"Lady Effie is an expert on Mr. Shakespeare's plays. We were talking about Edmund Kean's interpretation of Shylock. His Shylock never stands still, and there is no vacant pause in the action."

He nodded his agreement. "He is the embodiment of Shylock. Lady Euphemia, were you at the performance?"

"I arrived rather late. I am one of the only people in the audience who kept their eyes on the stage rather than the loge." Effie grabbed Anna's hand. "Congratulations to you both."

"Pardon, Lady Anna." The three turned to the footman. "You are needed at the banquet table."

Anna tried to see who was at the table, but her view was obstructed by the crowd.

"I had best go. You two go on. We're almost done for the night. I'll find you when I'm finished."

She had no idea what the problem could be. The event would be over presently, and the staff knew what needed to be done.

"What seems to be the problem?" She and the footman threaded their way through the crowd that was beginning to thin.

"A gentleman asked that I fetch you."

Her pace slowed. "Fetch me? Were those his exact words?"

"Yes, my lady. There he is. At the end of the table, his back to us."

She looked where he pointed. Richard.

"Did you want to speak to me?" She came up next to him.

He turned around.

"Here you are. You've led me on a merry chase. When I didn't find you at Raven Hall, I came here. I've come to fetch you. I have a place for the reception. You must come and see it."

"Not now." The last thing she wanted was to draw attention to themselves. "The Millers have made the library available. I'll talk to you about it tomorrow."

"No, no. I told them I would bring you now. We must at least look at it. It's not far." He raised his voice. People close by stared at him.

He reached for her hand, but Willbury took it first.

"Lady Anna said tomorrow."

"This is not your concern. Anna and I—"

"Are what? Don't embarrass yourself and tell me she's your fiancée when we all know that is not the truth."

"Please, both of you," she said, her voice just above an irate whisper. "There is no need to make a scene. Richard, it's late. Now is not the time to look at a venue. I know all the halls in the area. Which one is it?"

"You're correct, Anna. Now is not the time. I'll speak to you tomorrow. We'll look at it then." He turned to Willbury. "Your Grace." He gave a curt nod and withdrew.

"Are you certain you want to go anywhere with him? He makes me uneasy."

"I appreciate your concern. But it would be easier for me to look at the venue. He and I have had our ups and downs about this event."

Another deception? *Tell him what you found, what you know.* But if she told him, he would take over and not include her in getting to the truth. No, not yet. She was well on her way to proving she was more than a hostess, more than a wealthy man's daughter, even more than a lord's potential wife. This was her opportunity to prove her own self-worth.

Willbury hadn't taken his eyes off Richard until he walked out the door. Now, he gazed into her eyes. "Getting an event right is one thing. Letting you leave with him is another."

"This is for me to manage. Not you." Quietly she added, "You've been out of my life for nearly ten years, and I have learned to work things out myself."

"Anna."

She turned as the Millers came up to her.

"The evening was wonderful. We will have to begin planning for next year."

Willbury started to leave, but she took his hand to hold on to him for one more moment.

The corner of his lips quirked in amusement, and he whispered in her ear, "You are more than capable of managing Younge. I am regretting missing those ten years. I'll see you tomorrow at my reception."

He thanked the Millers for an enjoyable evening and left the library.

"You've repaired that nicely," Mrs. Bainbridge said as he walked across Westmore Commons with her and Barrington.

"I know Anna from ten years ago, the girl who was strong and capable. I also know that there are strong and capable men who have been duped by Spivey."

"And you want to protect her. That's who you are, but you can't suffocate her."

He knew the headmistress was correct. "I've spent the last ten years keeping people safe. Younge is nothing but an opportunist and a fraud. The more I find out about him, the more I want Anna to stay away from him."

They walked on toward the seminary.

"The few months Younge managed Aunt Adelaide's estate resulted in a disaster. It's not difficult to see his plan. Spivey and Richard are looking for power and money. They tried to get Aunt Adelaide's money, but they didn't get far.

"I think Spivey has turned his attention to the Ravencrofts. I didn't like the way he stared at Anna in the tearoom. Barrington, the judge, and I spoke about this the other day. Spivey has his protégé marry for money, then drains the wife's family dry." They stood at the seminary door. "Anna is their next target."

Chapter Nineteen

In the morning, Mrs. Cutler and several of the staff were busy loading the wagon for Willbury's reception. The day was unusually warm for late September. They decided to set up several tables outside. Although they had spent a good part of yesterday making The Willow ready for the reception, opening the garden for the event required them to transport several items from Raven Hall.

Mrs. Cutler hurried in, glancing around the area to make sure nothing remained behind. "That crate is the last of the lot to go on the wagon."

"I'll have it for you in a moment." Anna knelt, counting the tablecloths. "I'll just recount the cloths for the garden tables."

"Pardon, Lady Anna. Mr. Younge is here to see you. I've put him in the drawing room."

"Five, six, seven. I have no time to see Richard now. Eight…"

"Mr. Francis Younge, my lady."

Anna stood up. She hadn't seen Francis in years.

"Thank you, Mr. Cutler. Please tell him I'll be right there."

The butler nodded and withdrew.

"One minute," she called after him.

She bent over the crate and finished counting the cloths, checked off her list, then handed it to him.

"Help Mrs. Cutler with this crate and get it loaded. Also, give her the list. She will know what to do with it. I will be along later."

Anna hurried down the hall. If Francis had visited three weeks ago, his visit would have been a pleasant surprise, but after what she learned, her intuition told her his arrival was not a coincidence.

"Cousin Francis. How good to see you," she said as she walked in. From the dust on his coat and boots, he must have been riding hard. He opened his arms for a warm embrace.

"Let me look at you, Annie." He stood back and looked her up and down, "You have grown into a beautiful young woman. I know you make your parents proud."

His warmth and true nature put her at ease. His hairline had receded quite a bit since the last time she saw him. What hair he had left was mostly gray. He was drawn and sallow. A quick and disturbing thought filled her mind. Was Francis here to support Richard?

He put his arm around her shoulder, and they walked to the garden window. "This was always my favorite view. We have a lovely place on the Scottish border. It suits my wife to be near her kin, but I do miss you and your family."

"I'm glad to see you, too. But I have a feeling this is not a family visit."

He let her go. His jovial face remained kind, but it turned serious.

"I will get right to the point. I'm told you are helping Richard with his campaign. Is that true?"

She went to her folio and pulled out the letter, the one she believed was forged, and handed it to him.

"Read it, please. I think it answers your question."

Anna watched as he read the letter quickly, then handed it back to her.

"I never wrote this. If I wanted your family's help, I would have gone to your father. I don't mean any disrespect."

"None taken. I recently realized that Richard forged this letter."

"He's let certain people believe that you are marrying him. Powerful people. I came here to stop you. That was until I read about you and Willbury in the paper." Francis stared at her, weighing his decision. There was more.

"I see that I came for naught. But my reasons were good ones. I came to stop you for several reasons. One, he is not worthy of you. Two." He looked away, ashamed to tell her.

"That he is already married."

His head popped up. "You, you know?"

"Richard has been busy these last two weeks. He's lied to me about your support of his candidacy, he's led Willbury to believe that he and I are to be married while already having a wife, and…" She paused. "Well, there is more. It's all very damning."

Until she knew Francis's place in this game, she was not going to tell him about Richard's larceny. At least, not yet.

"Did he tell you that he was married?"

"He conveniently kept that to himself. While I am happy to help my family, people I am close with had their doubts about Richard. I, too, had doubts about him and decided to find out what he was up to. I came upon a letter from his wife, Grace, asking him to come home. His children needed him."

"Cousin Francis. The things Richard has done are all terrible, but that's not what brought you here."

"I thought your father was here. Mr. Cutler informed me he is in Newcastle." He paced in front of her, rubbing the back of his neck. "Richard sent me a letter saying he had a plan to reunite the family. He was going to marry you. Richard can be very unreasonable at times. I would never forgive myself if anything happened to you or those you love."

Anna heard his hidden meaning and tried to stay calm. Richard and Willbury had words. He was irrational enough to think he could confront him.

"We're family. Good or bad. We help and protect each other."

"As you can see, I am fine. Willbury is fine. We are going to The Willow. It is Willbury's first Sunday reception. Will you come along? Everyone will be there, and you are still the borough representative."

He peered out the door as if he could see The Willow. "I should speak to Willbury, give him my congratulations, and speak to him about young Saxton. An excellent choice for representative."

"You go on ahead. I'll see you there." She walked him to the door and waited until he was on his way.

She started up the stairs to get herself ready. She couldn't shake the sensation that Francis had more to say. Perhaps it was too much to tell her all at once. Perhaps after the reception. There was plenty of time.

Carriages made their way up the drive to The Willow and waited for their passengers to disembark. Mr. Forbes and his men managed to get the conveyances out of the way quickly to avoid an excessively long line.

In the grand foyer, Willbury, with Kaiah sitting quietly at his heel, stood with Mrs. Bainbridge, greeting the guests.

After the first half hour, the crush of people was down to a trickle.

"Your Grace, Mrs. Bainbridge." Mr. Barton brought them both a glass of wine after they greeted the last person.

"Mrs. Bainbridge, thank you for your assistance. Anna planned a wonderful event." He took a sip of wine. "I didn't see her arrive."

He gave a last worried look down the drive before Mr. Barton closed the door. He offered Mrs. Bainbridge his arm and started toward the garden with Kaiah trotting alongside them.

"It's early, I'm sure she's taking care of a last-minute detail or two. She'll be here soon." They stopped for a brief word with the Lord Mayor, then continued on.

"You know Anna loves you. And before you say anything, I know you have your differences."

"Not differences. In my driving desire to protect her, I blundered and told her only I can take care of her. I didn't do it to make myself important or to make her less of a person. I feared she was getting pulled into a situation she wasn't prepared to handle. One that I know does not play within the rules of the world to which she is accustomed. However, all I did was drive her away. I see it in her eyes." He let out a deep breath. "I'm afraid I may have made things worse. If she reacts the way I suspect, she may do something rash to prove me wrong."

"Have you told her you love her?"

He stroked Kaiah and looked sheepishly at Mrs. Bainbridge.

"No. I thought not. You planned to show her, to prove your love by protecting her. You are a brave and gallant knight, but you can better protect her by helping her protect herself. And do not think for one minute that is enough. A woman also needs to be told she is loved. Just as much as a man needs to hear it himself."

He and Mrs. Bainbridge walked through the drawing room doors and into the garden.

"Are you off duty?" Barrington came up to them. "Because I need a word in private with our host."

"You two have a nice chat. I will see you later."

"Thank you again, Mrs. Bainbridge. For everything." She walked off and joined a group of women at a nearby table.

"I've heard from Wilmore. He has been busy. He gathered the financial information you requested and found some interesting items. They're on your library desk."

"We can tackle that after everyone leaves." Willbury had a good idea what Wilmore found, and from Barrington's reaction, it appeared promising. Finally, some justice for Lloyd Saxton.

"Did I see you speaking with Francis Younge?" Barrington appeared as surprised as he was when the man arrived.

"Yes, his appearance was a surprise. He was pressed for time and wanted to wish me well. We spoke briefly about the election and confirmed his support for Ellis Saxton. Reports that he's supporting his son are greatly exaggerated. Francis mentioned he spoke to Anna before he came here. I had the distinct feeling that he had more to say, but we were interrupted when Judge Scofield arrived. I thought I would continue our conversation, but I saw him leave. I suppose all in good time."

"Are you two talking business again?" Mrs. Barrington came up to them. "Enough. This is your party. No more business or politics. It's time to enjoy your new responsibilities."

Two hours later, the last of the guests were gone. The tables were cleared, and items packed to be returned to Raven Hall. Barrington and Mrs. Bainbridge sat across from Willbury, who drummed his fingers on the table. Kaiah sat at his feet.

"Your Grace." A Raven Hall footman ran from the house. Mr. Barton close behind him.

Willbury leapt up as if propelled by an explosion and nearly turned the table over in the process. The dog stood by him.

"My lord, Mr. Cutler sent me. Lady Anna and Mrs. Cutler went with Mr. Younge to look at a hall and have not returned. Mr. Cutler has taken a few men and gone to find them at the old town hall in Springhill on the Harrogate Road."

Fear and anger knotted his insides. Why didn't she listen? He told her to stay away from Richard. If he hadn't been so foolish. If he hadn't made his demands. He knew the girl well enough to know the woman. She took his words as a challenge. This was his doing.

"Mr. Barton, a coach will arrive presently. See that Mrs. Castleton is settled in. I will return as soon as possible."

He and Kaiah headed for the stable.

"Honoria, take the gig. Tell Peter where I've gone. He'll gather the men and bring the militia. Willbury will need more than the dog to help him." Barrington stared at Willbury's retreating back. "I'm going with him."

Chapter Twenty

The last of the guest's carriages rolled out of the stable yard. The men were gathering to enjoy the last of the cider sent over by the kitchen.

"Forbes!" he called as he reached the stable.

The men turned at the urgency in His Grace's voice.

"I need five able-bodied men to come with me. Lady Anna and Mrs. Cutler are missing."

The head groom gave out orders like an army sergeant. Organized tumult followed as men grabbed what they needed and saddled their mounts. While Willbury explained the situation to Forbes, a groom brought out his horse.

Willbury mounted up. In the midst of the chaos, the stallion tossed its mane and pawed the ground impatient to be off.

Willbury's soft words and gentle touches calmed the beast. With Barrington and Kaiah next to them, they waited at the front of the line. The small troop was saddled and ready in minutes.

"Lady Anna and Mrs. Cutler were going to the old town hall in Springhill. Rather than take the main road, we'll cut across the old Benson farm and take the road from there. Mr. Cutler and several men from Raven Hall are already on their way."

They rode hard across the field, Kaiah keeping up with the troop. They passed the deserted Benson farmhouse and overgrown garden. Forbes sent one of the men to investigate the farm buildings. They were empty.

Withered grass stretched across the deserted farm and rustled in the late September air. They continued past the farm to get to the road north toward Springhill.

Kaiah raced on. She was too far ahead of them for Willbury to call her back. She'd find them soon enough. But before they got to the road, Kaiah raced back and forth barking for his attention.

Willbury brought the men around and followed the dog. In the distance, he made out kicked up dust, a group of riders. As they got closer, he recognized Cutler and the Raven Hall men. He quickened their pace.

They came up to Cutler, who stood next to a disabled carriage, the Ravencroft crest on the door.

"Your Grace, we found the carriage. The wheel is off. There's no sign of the women or Richard. Only this." Cutler handed Willbury a shawl. "Lady Anna was wearing it when they went with Mr. Younge."

Willbury examined it and seethed. He showed it to Barrington. It was stained with blood.

"This isn't the way to Springhill." Barrington's eyes swept up then down the road. "This road circles back toward Sommer-by-the-Sea."

"Yes, to a remote part of the village. Where is he taking them?" Willbury stood holding the shawl and surveyed the area. "He could have taken them in any direction."

Kaiah tried to get the shawl from Willbury.

"Not now." He pulled the shawl away. But she was insistent.

Barrington took the shawl and presented it to Kaiah.

The dog sniffed the material. She jumped into the carriage, then came out sniffing the ground. She went in several directions, each time coming back to the carriage. She followed a scent into the meadow. After going some distance, Kaiah barked and continued on.

The men mounted up and followed her.

"She's going toward the village," Barrington shouted to Willbury. They rode on.

As they came over a rise, they found Kaiah pacing along the banks of a stream.

"Has she lost the scent?" Mr. Cutler asked.

"Give her time. She'll pick up the scent again."

Kaiah paced up and down the stream, stopped to sniff, then continued on until she made a decision and crossed.

Willbury and the others followed.

The scent must have gotten stronger. Kaiah trotted along but, without warning, came to a halt.

There was movement up ahead. Kaiah took off running. The troop surged forward at a full gallop.

Mr. Cutler brought up his horse and jumped off as his wife ran into his arms.

"You've never looked so good." She buried her head in his chest.

Barrington and Willbury stood anxiously at their side.

"What happened?" Cutler tried to move the bandage she wore around her head.

"You gave us all a fright." Half in anticipation, half in dread, Willbury asked, "What happened, and where is Lady Anna?"

She tried to pull out of her husband's arms. "We must help her."

"Yes, Martha, we will. We can't until you tell us what happened." Her husband removed the bandage and found a head wound.

She pushed his hand away.

"Mr. Younge arrived at Raven Hall as we got into the carriage. He insisted Lady Anna look at the hall in Springhill. She relented and said we would go with him and from there leave for The Willow.

"When he kept going rather than take the road to Springhill, Lady Anna grabbed the reins. We struggled until the carriage slid off the road, and the wheel dislodged." She gazed at her husband who examined the gash on her forehead. "That's when I hit my head." Her attention shifted back to Lord Reese and Willbury. "Lady Anna said we wouldn't go any farther. He said his house was up ahead."

She looked at her husband. "His father was there, tied up. His head was bleeding." She turned to the duke. "Lady Anna took control. She tore a sheet and made a bandage for me and one for Mr. Younge. I thought Richard would get violent, but thankfully, he didn't."

"Thankfully, you have a hard head, Mrs. Cutler. The bleeding's stopped." The butler held his wife close and breathed a sigh of relief.

"He locked us all in the bedroom. Lady Anna decided I was to leave through the window and get help. I escaped as Richard came back into the room. I went through the gate in the garden wall, then ran as fast as I could."

She gave them the particulars about the house and the service lane on the other side of the wall.

"You are very brave, Mrs. Cutler." Willbury turned to her husband. "Take her back to Raven Hall and see to her injury. We will follow as soon as we have Lady Anna."

With the Cutlers and the Raven Hall men safely away, Willbury and the others continued on. They came to the street where the house was located and navigated the mucked and muddy lane.

Kaiah sniffed down the wall and raised her head when she found the garden door.

"Good girl." Willbury ruffled the dog's head. They both slipped through. Keeping low to the ground, they made their way to the bedroom window. Willbury peeked over the sill. He stared at Richard's back and into Anna's eyes.

There were no tell-tale signs of injury. For that he was thankful. Nor did she appear overly stressed. To his relief, she was aware and alert.

The corners of her mouth twitched. Her attention shifted to Richard.

Willbury evaluated the situation. Capturing Richard without harm coming to Anna or Francis was his primary goal. He had to wait for the right opportunity. While he and Kaiah stood watching at the window, the others circled around to the front of the house.

"Richard, I'm going to get up, take your father, and go back to Raven Hall." She had already freed Francis.

"No. You are both staying here." Richard rummaged through a cabinet drawer.

She gave him a withering stare and turned to Francis and helped him to his feet.

Willbury couldn't wait any longer. He had no idea what lengths Richard would go to in order to save himself.

"Don't move. Either of you." Richard threatened her, waving a knife.

There wasn't any way Willbury could get through the window and disarm Richard without risking either Anna or Francis. He glanced at Kaiah. All he needed was a distraction to give him time to get through the window. The dog was his answer. He moved to the side and signaled the dog to go into the room.

Kaiah jumped through the window, barking and growling. She attacked Richard, going after his hand with the knife. Standing on her hind legs, the dog was almost as tall as him and more agile.

Richard screamed and struggled to no avail. The knife fell out of his hand as Richard tumbled to the floor.

With his arms covering his face, screaming for help, Kaiah stood over him, growling with her teeth bared.

Anna moved quickly and kicked the knife out of reach.

"Sit." She sat at Willbury's command as Forbes and the others broke down the door and rushed into the room.

Willbury lifted Richard up by his collar. The anger that had built up over the last several days, the threat to Anna's safety, all came together. He ached to pummel him.

Anna touched his arm. "He's not worth it. Let Lord Reese and Judge Scofield deal with him. There is something more important you need to see."

"Forbes. Hold him." His man took Richard and bound his hands. Richard did not go quietly. He screamed and made his demands.

"This is Richard's house." She took Willbury to the cellar door.

"Where are you going? You can't go down there," Richard demanded. "Willbury is a hateful man, Anna. He abandoned his wife and child and plays the lord and master. Don't say I didn't warn you."

"Mr. Forbes, if he doesn't stop complaining, stuff his mouth."

"It would be my pleasure, Lady Anna." Forbes grabbed a cloth from the table ready for Richard's next salvo.

Anna took Willbury's hand and brought him down the cellar steps.

She pointed to the velvet pouch. "Behind that, you'll find your great-uncle's sword. I didn't look in all the crates, but they have the Willbury crest. I do not think these were gifts."

"I won't ask you how you know about this." He went from crate to crate, examining its contents.

"You heard Richard just now. It's not the first time I've heard that claim from him. You would never…" Her voice trailed off. "That is not you, and it was his claims about your character that led me to believe you were right about him. I needed to prove to myself what else he lied about. I was going to tell you what I found after your reception. Here we are instead."

He swept her up into his arms and kissed her soundly.

"The thought that you were at Richard's mercy—"

"You should have more faith in me. You were the one who taught me how to defend myself. Luckily, Kaiah and you made it unnecessary. I enjoy your embrace, but I don't want to stay in this house any longer than I have to."

He draped his arm around her shoulder. They went out the cellar door to the garden. The men gathered in the yard.

"We'll bring Richard to The Willow. I'd rather return immediately than question him here."

"Lord Reese's men arrived as we were fixing the carriage wheel. They brought the carriage. It's in the lane." Forbes motioned to the garden wall.

"Barrington, Lady Anna found several missing Willbury items in the cellar."

"I'll have my men go through the house and bring the Willbury items back to The Willow." Barrington nodded to his men.

Anna got into the carriage with Francis. Kaiah jumped in and sat between them.

Willbury was about to ask her if she could handle the carriage but thought better of it.

He walked his horse close to the wagon. "I wanted to talk to you before we got back to The Willow, but it will have to wait."

"Is it important? I can step down—" She pulled up the carriage.

"No. No. Like you, I'd rather be rid of this place. We'll talk later."

The ride back was uneventful. Anna easily handed the carriage and brought it up to the door of The Willow. Mr. Barton came out to help Francis down.

"Your Grace, Mrs. Castleton and her daughter have arrived along with the Duke of Oakdene."

Chapter Twenty-One

Mrs. Castleton? Anna's head snapped around and glared at him. Had Richard told her the truth all along?

He nodded to the butler, took Anna by the hand, and started toward the house.

"I'm going back to Raven Hall." Anna tried to pull away from him.

"No. This is the last of my half-truths. Trust me. I will not stop you if you want to leave after you hear me out. I have nothing to hide, especially from you."

They walked into the drawing room. In front of the fireplace stood a tall statuesque woman wearing a stylish pelisse, holding a young girl that looked remarkably like Willbury. Oakdene rose as she entered.

"Lady Marianna Ravencroft, I'd like you to meet Elyse, Lucian's wife and their daughter, Giselle."

Elyse stepped toward her with a warm greeting. "I have heard so much about you that I think I know you. Giselle, come say hello to your Uncle Fraser, then you can play with Kaiah."

Giselle dipped a curtsy, gave her a smile, then turned to her mother. "Now?"

"Yes, go." Elyse turned to Anna. "Children."

"She is lovely. She looks like her father. You are Willbury's well-kept secret." Anna gazed at him, but it was Oakdene who had the answer.

"That is my fault. Elyse worked with Lucian during the war. She provided him with somewhat sensitive information."

"When my husband died, I thought our mission was over, and I had lost my protection. Giselle was only months old. I tried to continue without him, but I did not have the contacts. That's when Fraser proposed his idea. No one could tell the two brothers apart. It was a perfect solution. Fraser took up his brother's work for the crown by becoming Lucian until the mission was completed." Elyse looked at Willbury. "We both mourned Lucian as well as celebrated his life."

"Elyse was under suspicion." Oakdene, Barrington's brother Edward, went to her side. "We had to be careful. Injured, we brought Willbury back to England first. Garrett Fletcher worked with Elyse and Willbury. He stayed with them until we could bring them to England. It took some work to get Elyse and Giselle out."

"If it wasn't for both of them, I don't know what would have happened to us. But we are here to congratulate the new Duke of Willbury."

"I didn't do anything special but outlive the four or so others in the line of succession." Willbury chuckled. "I am glad you're here. Where is Garrett? Isn't he with you?"

"I would never let them travel alone." Fletcher, a protégé of Lord Oakdene, entered the room. "Good evening, Lady Anna. I see you've met my wife and daughter. How good it is to see you."

"It's good to see you as well. Your parents are well?"

"Yes, we're off to see them. Elyse and I are celebrating our anniversary. We've been married three months." Fletcher turned to his wife, his gaze tender and sweet. "We couldn't get married until Elyse and Giselle were in England. She was the wife of a war hero, Lucian Castleton. We survived bigger obstacles. We're here, at last."

"Congratulations." Anna and Willbury looked at the happy couple. There was something binding in their relationship that was undefinable but palpably there. Anna felt privileged to be with them.

"We nursed each other's wounds, some more grievous than others. There was a time when we were a sorry lot." Fletcher peeked at Giselle, fast asleep and cuddled with Kaiah.

Fletcher picked up his daughter. "We're on our way to my family in Newcastle. Fortunately, Barrington has found need for a man in Newcastle. I'll be working with Wilmore." He looked at Elyse, then at Willbury and Anna. "We'll be back for the Harvest Ball. But now, we must go."

Willbury and Anna saw them to their carriage and said their good-byes. As they pulled away, Lord Reese arrived. He alighted from his mount and, with his brother, went into the library to look at Wilmore's documents.

"I hope you understand that I couldn't say anything," Willbury said to Anna. "Not even to you."

"Some half-truths are forgivable."

"Richard's declaration startled me. The only people who know about Elyse are the Barringtons, Fletcher, and me. I can't believe they would break their silence."

"I'm certain they didn't. I suspect it's a coincidence. Richard could be blaming you for what he did, abandon his family."

They entered the library. The two Barrington brothers were at the desk amid papers.

"Richard had several crates full of Willbury wine. We found the missing money pouch, no money, and the late duke's sword. We also found a pair of candlesticks and various pieces of jewelry along with the duke's gold pocket watch."

Barrington handed Wilmore's papers to Willbury. He studied them.

"This is worse than we thought," Willbury said.

"Yes, I agree. Wilmore traced the money. There is a good case for fraud and theft, but it implicates Spivey, not Younge." Oakdene rummaged through the papers and pulled out one giving it to Willbury.

"But we found the missing pouch, the silver, and…" Anna turned to Willbury. "Oakdene must be wrong."

"Edward and I will bring Richard to Scofield on charges of kidnapping you, Mrs. Cutler, and his own father. The judge can order him put in the dungeon until we can get the militia to bring him to Harrogate." Barrington took the papers from Willbury and put them into the folio.

"There is an indication that he stole from Her Grace, but I don't see where there is evidence that he cannot wiggle his way out of. Possession perhaps," Barrington said to Anna. "I know it's not fair."

Forbes brought a restrained Richard into the library.

"He's right, you know. You cannot prove anything." Richard gloated. "I have no idea how any of those things got into my cellar. My wife, now that's another story. Grace must have put them there to put the blame on me. She was a servant at the Willow and knew the ways of the servants' stairs. She told me how she could get from room to room without anyone knowing. She did it all the time. It's how she was able to visit me while I lived in the cottage right under Mrs. Cutler's nose. She never knew a thing."

"He has a point." The Duke of Oakdene tossed down the pencil he had in his hand.

Standing behind the Barringtons with Willbury at her side, Anna listened and seethed until she couldn't stay quiet a moment longer.

"Grace may have shown you the servants' stairs, but she didn't take this." She reached into the bodice of her dress and took out the brooch. "The duchess pinned this to her nightrail every night since her husband's passing. According to Mrs. Bainbridge, she saw Her Grace that evening and commented on the pin."

Richard sat in front of her with vengeful eyes.

"And before you blame the theft on Grace, she wasn't in service the evening the duchess died. The gem was ripped off her nightrail. And let me remind you that *you* gave it to me."

Richard's smug expression turned into a worried gaze that went from one person to the next.

"You used the servants' stairs and entered the duchess's room through the jib door." Barrister Willbury intoned his summation in a voice that could shake the chamber in the Old Bailey.

"You can't prove that." Richard's voice was filled with defiance and more than a hint of challenge.

"The servants' stairs are not maintained. They're thickly covered with dust, with footprints, only one set. Everyone wears their shoes down in a different manner. All I need to do is match your shoes to the footprint by the jib door in my aunt's room."

Richard sat back and winced at Willbury's words.

Anna could tell from his shamefaced expression their version of that evening was the true one.

"Taking the silver, the sword, and even my great-uncle's watch was not enough," Willbury continued his summation. "You planned to steal the gem from a dying woman. But you didn't count on Kaiah. You locked her in the closet, and when you ran from her room you pushed Her Grace down the stairs and—"

"No. I swear. I didn't hurt her. She tripped and tumbled."

"Did you cause her to fall? Did you come to her aid?" Anna's low and confident voice rang with determination. "Or did she watch you pull her most precious gem from her nightrail then leave her there alone and dying?"

Richard was too startled by Anna's words to say anything.

"One last thing." Anna wasn't finished. "How did Spivey know how Lady Adelaide died?"

"How should I know—"

"You should know." Willbury flashed a glance at Anna who nodded for him to continue. "He told me at the tearoom that the steward told him."

All the pieces of the puzzle fell into place.

"Forbes, put him in the carriage." Willbury waved his hand in dismissal.

Tired, Anna gazed out the window as Forbes removed Richard. The sky was dove gray with a subtle hint of purple, just enough to announce the coming sunset. She was glad everything was over.

Barrington rose and stood in front of Anna. "Well done, Lady Anna. You may have missed your calling. You plan beautiful parties, but you would make a brilliant barrister. Come, Edward, we'll take Lady Anna's first case to Judge Scofield."

The Barringtons took their leave, but his words echoed in her head.

"He's correct. We wouldn't be able to prosecute Richard for either crime without your evidence. Not only Aunt Adelaide's death, but there is a very good possibility that your findings, along with the original testimony, may be what we need to have Lloyd Saxton's conviction expunged. That, Lady Marianna Ravencroft, is better than well done. That, my very dear and lovely Anna, is extraordinary."

Gathered in his arms, he held her snugly, tucking her head against his chest.

"I don't know when I've been more scared," he whispered into her hair. "Seeing you in that room at Richard's mercy and having to wait was torture."

"You were scared. I was angry with his lies and manipulation." She lifted her head, and he kissed her lips, a small tender kiss. "Then I looked into your eyes, Your Grace, and I found more strength. You gave me the strength I needed."

"Fraser, please. I've missed the way you say my name."

He kissed her again, deeply, passionately. Her body tingled and thrummed, but it was more than carnal pleasure. They teased each other, argued, and even had words, but with all that, they remained for each other. She knew whatever happened, they always would.

A deep breath filled her with his scent of lavender and citrus. Laying her hand on his chest, she felt his heartbeat faster, and his broad muscular chest swelled.

The hum of activity as the staff set the garden back together faded, shadows lengthened, and dusk took hold. They didn't move. They stood in the darkening room, content to hold one another.

Moments ticked past as his gaze seared hers. Her fingers combed the pesky lock of hair that fell over his eyes back into place.

"I tried to imagine you wearing your powdered wig in the Old Bailey with this out-of-control lock of hair."

Fraser's laugh was soft and sensual. He braced his hand on the wall behind her, then leaned in, closing the distance between them to a few inches. His breath brushed against her face. "How did it look?"

"Quite fetching."

His knuckles traced down the side of her face. Three more heartbeats passed before he whispered, "Not as fetching as you in your lavender gown at the theater. You took my breath away."

His touch was like velvet as his fingers slid down her neck. He showered kisses against her lips and her jaw, followed by slow shivery kisses down her neck, stopping at the hollow of her throat.

Her breath caught from the intoxication, as if she'd had too much wine. She didn't want him to stop.

The back of his hand brushed above her breasts. Her heart banged against her chest, and a soft sound escaped her lips.

His clever hands slipped up her arms and worked their way to her back. His touch was suddenly almost unbearable in its tenderness.

He cupped her head, his face so close she saw the smoldering passion in his eyes. He covered her mouth with his own, capturing her lips in a fierce, hot possession, sending her stomach into a wild swirl that built into an all-consuming desire.

Each kiss sent shock waves through her body and brought her to a place where only they belonged. She yearned for him, for something that she couldn't control, and by all that was holy, she didn't want to.

She returned his kiss with a need she didn't try to hide. She opened her lips and let him in. With a hunger matching her own, he took possession and explored her gift. He kissed her thoroughly, passionately, completely igniting an ache with that one unforgettable kiss.

Artful fingers brushed over her skin, over her rapidly pounding pulse, and made her tremble. He traced the contour of her breast, and she felt the touch all the way through her.

A sudden thrilling, panic-stricken moment ran rampant in her veins until she surrendered, only to have it disappear in a burst of heat.

Fraser held her close. If he hadn't, she was sure she would have flown apart.

"My dear wonderful Mari-an-na." He whispered her name as if it were a prayer.

Chapter Twenty-Two

One week later

With the music of the Harvest Ball in the background, Anna and Fraser stole away for a quiet moment in the conservatory at The Willow.

"You took chances you shouldn't have taken."

"Did I thank you for hosting the ball?"

"Don't change the subject."

"Chances? To your thinking, perhaps." She turned and faced him. "Sometimes people must do what has to be done. It is their destiny. No one else's. I thought I was proving myself to you. I wasn't. I was proving to myself that I was capable. You already knew. But enough about that nightmare.

"We should get back to your guests."

He gave her a long, tender kiss on her lips. "If we must, but I would much rather stay here." He let out a deep sigh.

"To your guests, Your Grace." Anna rose and pulled him to his feet.

He cringed at the appellation and followed her to the door. "You have done a wonderful job turning The Willow into an autumn wonderland."

"I'm glad you approve. It's one of my many skills."

They laughed as they entered the ballroom. Candlelight set the myriad of elegant gowns sparkling. A quartet played while the guests danced. Fraser went to the dais as the music ended. The conductor tapped for attention.

All eyes focused on their host.

"I want to take this opportunity to welcome everyone to this year's Gold and Glitter Harvest Ball."

The guests applauded.

"I also want to thank you for welcoming me back to Sommer-by-the-Sea. To answer a question that many of you have asked, The Willow will be my permanent residence. I plan to visit London only when I must."

The guests laughed.

He gestured to Anna to join him. She shook her head and moved away. He stepped toward her, took her hand, and drew her in front of everyone.

"All of you have read Mr. Hawkins' article in the Sommer Sentinel about Lady Anna and me."

She tried to pull her hand away, but he held it tight.

"I am here to declare"—he turned to her—"when I was last in Newcastle, before your parents departed for London, I asked for your hand."

The guests were quiet.

"Your father trusts you to make the right decision and will support it. So, my fate is in your hands."

A sigh went up in the crowd, especially from where the majority of ladies stood.

"However, as a barrister, I cannot leave it at that. I must state my case."

"'Hear ye, hear ye,'" called the men on the other side of the room, sending everyone laughing.

"My attributes… I am someone who has known you since childhood and does not hold that against you."

Even she could not hide her laughter.

"I am someone who has felt strongly about justice and the law. I am someone who is fit and somewhat handsome and, I'm told, I am very humble."

The guest's polite laughter turned into full guffaws.

"My faults…"

Everyone quieted down.

"I have fallen hopelessly in love with a woman who challenges me to think and to be the best that I can be. Above all else, she is devoted to family. I am sorry to say in the past I thought that, in order to protect her, I could not be totally truthful."

"I say to you, here and now, Marianna Ravencroft, I give you my word, I give you myself, and I give you no more half-truths. What else do you want? Name it and it is yours." He held her hand tenderly.

The guests made not a sound.

"I need but one thing to make me complete." She gazed deeply into Fraser's beautiful blue-green eyes. "*Mon bijou. Mon Coeur.* My heart. My jewel. I want you."

They sealed their oath with a kiss.

The End

Thank you for taking the time to read The Lady and the Barrister (The Return to the Ladies of Sommer-by-the-Sea, Book 1). And thank you in advance for sharing your enjoyment of this story (or my other stories) with fellow readers by leaving a review on Amazon. Long or short, detailed or to the point, I read all the reviews and greatly appreciate you for writing one!

To keep up to date with new stories, where you can find me, and my friends, please consider subscribing to my newsletter (and receive a free book as a gift.)

The story continues in Book Two, *The Lady and the Earl*

The Lady and the Earl

A woman's manipulating behavior is a prescription for disaster.
But for whom?

Lady Harriet Manning is a busy woman. Aside from giving her time to the Ladies Auxiliary, she assists her father, the renowned physician Bertram Manning as his very competent protégé. While societal protocol prevents her from practicing, the stubborn Harriet has established a clinic for those in need. Much to her mother's chagrin, Lady Harriet has no time to attract a husband. Does Harriet expect the perfect man to simply appear at her door?

On his way back to London from the Scottish Highlands, the dashing, and a bit reckless Lord Gavin, the Earl of Brookville has a riding accident. He's brought to the clinic where Harriet sees to his injuries. Brookville's convalescence provides time for healing and without any pretenses, the opening of hearts to a loving relationship.

The Mannings are shocked when they bring their patient home to London and learn he is the son of the Duke of Whippany, and Lady Whippany is an old childhood friend of her mother. Encouraged by her mother, Harriet stifles her medical abilities and plays the prim and proper lady. She will do all she can to fit into his world. Harriet and Gavin announce their engagement. However, the ton and Daphne Willis in particular, have a different plan.

When a political guest at a ball takes ill and no one in attendance is able to help him, Harriet steps forward and saves the man. She's overheard telling Gavin the illness is not natural but appears to be an attempt on the man's life.

London is in an uproar at Harriet's secret medical ability and her extraordinary claim of attempted murder. Daphne Willis works against them determined to doom their budding romance through all types of trickery. Will Harriet and Gavin's love survive in the wilds of London?

The Lady and Her Quill

Lady Alicia Hartley's head kept telling her to stop loving him,
But her heart couldn't let him go.

"It's very easy to get involved with our characters feelings in this historical romance. Both are right and wrong, and when they realize that the excitement and adventure really starts." ~ Petula, Goodreads

Renowned author Lady Alicia Hartley has lost her muse after a bad review. She blames it all on the author JC Melrose. A chance encounter with a handsome, witty Justin Caulfield has her heart racing, and her muse seemingly back. Is he her savior or her worst nightmare?

The recently retired Captain Justin Caulfield is facing his own demons. As gifted author JC Melrose, his stories honor men who died at the hand of one man. His only focus is to avenge their deaths, that is, until he meets and falls in love with Lady Alicia.

The two authors take on a writing challenge based on a story of stolen gold taken from the newspaper headlines all to determine the better writer. While researching the story, Lady Alicia is captured by the thieves' ringleader. Can Lady Alicia turn this mystery into an award-winning story? Can Justin save his real-life heroine? Can they both overcome their own challenges for a happily ever after?

Chapter One

Lady Alicia Hartley clutched the heavy parcel under her arm and hurried along Fleet Street through the thick fog. She took scant notice of the people rushing past her or the church bells chiming noon. New ideas fluttered and flittered through her mind. Success had led to opportunities she never dreamt possible until now. Her lips pursed as she tried to suppress a satisfied smile.

Caution. The small inner voice broke through her dreaming and her brows knitted together. Don't be reckless.

Alicia rubbed the amber stone she wore around her neck. The pendant was a gift from her father.

Confidence is everything, though, was one of Mrs. Bainbridge's guiding principles.

It started with Miss Whitlock. Since Alicia was a little girl, Miss Greta Whitlock had been her governess. Alicia was fond of the tall, pleasant woman who at times was more like an older sister. Some of her best memories were sitting in the window seat in the attic room, staring at the sea and just talking about hopes, aspirations, dreams, and well, everything. Nothing was prohibited. If anything, the woman encouraged her to be an independent thinker and draw her own conclusions.

Alicia soon became proficient in drawing, needlecraft, music, and dance. While only a passing knowledge of French and Italian was expected, Alicia excelled past songs and snippets of poems and stories presented in the romantic languages. Her natural curiosity eventually drove her to acquire fluency in both, and proficiency in Greek and Latin.

Her schooling included the practical study of household management that went beyond managing the staff and counting the silver, but also included training in hiring, purchasing, and gardening.

Decorum ruled a lady's life from her core to her habits. Nothing less was tolerated. Everything she did was scrutinized and criticized, but Miss Whitlock had done her job well.

They spent hours in the attic at her desk and looked forward to those days her father was not home. He agreed she could use his library when it wasn't occupied. She sat at the large table, surrounded by books, and enjoyed their sweet, musky scent.

Of all the subjects, her true love was writing – taking the actions, colors, sounds, and emotions of imaginary people and places she conjured in her mind and translating them into words for others to read and enjoy.

She had all but driven Miss Whitlock dizzy with her thirst for knowledge and her quest to improve her writing.

By the time she was fifteen, she mastered all the acceptable subjects a young woman was expected to learn and others some people would think unnecessary, a waste of time, or worse, scandalous.

With her parents' agreement, her governess sometimes submitted her essays to the village paper, the Sommer Sentinel. Mr. Leon Hawkins, the elderly owner, enjoyed her short story about Margaret's Miracle, a long-held folk tale about the village mayor's daughter Margaret and a Scottish trader. It was a reflective essay that spoke about the tale and introduced ideas based on facts she researched.

Hawkins also printed her more creative pieces. One in particular, her story that featured an upper-class lady and her plight in London society, had been very well received.

"You make me proud," Miss Whitlock had said, standing next to her at the library table, her hands clasped in front of her.

Proud. Alicia glowed brighter than the light from the oil lamp at the compliment.

"Put your books away and bundle up. It's bitterly cold out, and we're going to the tearoom today."

It was an innocent excursion. One they had made many times before. One she thoroughly enjoyed. Or was it the biscuits that drew her there?

When they arrived at the tearoom, Miss Whitlock led the way to a table by the window, where they joined another woman.

"Honoria, I'd like to introduce you to Lady Alicia Hartley."

Miss Whitlock turned to her.

"Lady Alicia, this is my dear friend, Mrs. Honoria Bainbridge."

Everyone knew Mrs. Bainbridge – if not in person, then most definitely by reputation. She was the head of the Sommer-by-the-Sea Female Seminary, an elite school that every girl in the district, if not all of England, wanted to attend.

One didn't apply to the seminary. Admittance was only by Mrs. Bainbridge's personal invitation.

She and Miss Whitlock took their seats. Tea was already laid and waiting for them. At first, Alicia thought she would be a silent observer and given an opportunity to occasionally add her voice to the conversation.

Instead, she sat at the table as if she was a pane of glass, one both women saw right through. As tea progressed, she became anxious, and she had no idea why.

"Lady Alicia." Pulled from her star-gazing, she faced Mrs. Bainbridge. "Have you seen the London papers? Edmund Kean has signed a contract with Drury Lane. He is to play Shylock in The Merchant of Venice. They are expecting a comedy," Mrs. Bainbridge said as she picked up her teacup. "What do you think of the play?"

It was a straightforward question.

One she was prepared for. She had studied Shakespeare and knew the play. "To me, the play is a drama, especially when Portia, disguised as a lawyer, begs Shylock to show mercy to Antonio. Her speech on the quality of mercy is dramatic and moving." Alicia took a breath and leaned forward, eager to go on. "The characters are sensitive and engaging. I don't see this play as a comedy. Although, I do think there are scenes where Shakespeare inserts comic elements to provide relief for the story's tension. But is the play a comedy? Not to me."

Mrs. Bainbridge smiled and gazed at her thoughtfully, then turned to Miss Whitlock.

"With the cold temperatures this last month, the Thames has frozen. There are plans for a frost fair between Blackfriars Bridge and London Bridge on the first of February." Mrs. Bainbridge set down her teacup and sighed. "I was a little girl when they had the last one."

Alicia really didn't want to talk about Shakespeare or the frost fair. She stared out the window at the cold gray sky and willed herself to stay in her seat.

"I read your story in the Sommer Sentinel."

Alicia whipped her head around and again faced Mrs. Bainbridge.

"Your story, the experience of a young upper-class woman who must navigate London society for the first time and falls in love with a social superior, was very good. I thoroughly enjoyed the way you re-created the social world. Your characters are sensitive and engaging. I like the way you let your reader experience their distress and tenderness.

"The conflict is well-planned and given with enough context to maintain a good pace and keep your reader turning pages. You are a good storyteller."

Alicia felt her face flush at the compliment. "Thank you, Mrs. Bainbridge. I'm glad you enjoyed the story."

"I do see room for growth."

Alicia stared at the woman and tamped down her annoyance. What was wrong with her writing?

She didn't think the headmistress would wait long to tell her.

"Draw out the conversations. Just because you know where it is going does not mean your reader does. And give a little more exposition within the narrative itself as an anchor."

"It is very kind of you to give me some direction. I will certainly keep your comments in mind."

"I expect you will. I see a young person eager to succeed. You will, you know. You are a gifted storyteller."

Mrs. Bainbridge gave her a smile, not one of those smiles that didn't reach the eyes, but a smile that came from her heart.

Alicia took a biscuit and finished her tea. She gave Miss Whitlock a fleeting glance. Her governess sat proudly by as she engaged in a conversation with Mrs. Bainbridge.

She liked her governess, but she wanted to learn more. In truth, she longed to be under Mrs. Bainbridge's tutelage. The headmistress worked with her students to create a plan filled with courses that surpassed anything Miss Whitlock could teach. Some were usually only available to men.

Mrs. Bainbridge's words kept repeating in her head.

You are a gifted storyteller.

With tea over and the snow beginning to fall, they said their good-byes and departed.

"What do you think of Mrs. Bainbridge?" Miss Whitlock asked as they walked along the river.

"She's an excellent judge of writing talent."

Miss Whitlock stared at her for a heartbeat or two before she burst out laughing. "Yes, she is," she concluded. "And I think she gave you excellent advice."

Mr. Dodd, the butler, opened the door as they reached it.

Alicia and Miss Whitlock went into the drawing room, laughing like schoolgirls. The soft scent of violet on the air announced her mother was present.

"Did you have a nice outing?" Lady Hartley said, looking over her spectacles as she stitched a sampler.

"It was wonderful. We had tea with Mrs. Bainbridge. And I was careful, I didn't spill my cup and I only took one biscuit."

Lady Hartley smiled and put down her stitching. "Yes, I know you can be quite civil when you put your mind to it."

"Mrs. Bainbridge complimented me on my essay that was in the Sentinel."

"Then she must have good literary taste," her mother said. "Before I forget, you received a letter."

"It must be from Hattie in London. She told me she'd write to tell me when she was returning to Sommer-by-the-Sea." Alicia took the dispatch from the salver and opened the letter.

She took a seat next to her mother, read the contents, then stared at the note without saying a word.

"Alicia, is anything wrong? I've never seen you so quiet," her mother said, glancing at Miss Whitlock.

Alicia looked at her governess, then her mother.

"What is it?" her mother asked.

"It's an invitation." Her heart was beating so loud she was sure her mother could hear it. She lifted her chin. "Mrs. Bainbridge has invited me to be a student at the Sommer-by-the-Sea Female Seminary."

Looking back, she had no idea that tea with Mrs. Bainbridge would change her life. That was seven years ago. She spent five wonderful years at the Sommer Female Seminary learning everything she could. Now, two years later, she still heard Mrs. Bainbridge's words warning caution.

She clutched the parcel to her chest. This completed project was a good one. Better than her last. As soon as she presented it to Mr. Caulfield, he too would be enthusiastic.

Remain calm. Be gracious and pleasant but remain firm.

By the time she had mentally repeated the words several times, her doubts quieted. Of course, Caulfield would bargain. She would remind him their past achievements were for the most part her doing. She no longer wanted to sell her story to Caulfield Publishing for a fee and receive nothing beyond that. Her books sold well and made a profit, but only for Caulfield.

The sales gave her the confidence to ask for a change in their financial arrangement on this last book in her contract. She would gladly pay all the production costs for publication. Caulfield Publishing would distribute them and get ten percent from the profits, a reasonable and more equitable financial arrangement. It would also give her more control of her work. She pressed her parcel closer to her chest. If he wouldn't budge, there was the letter that arrived in yesterday's post.

How could he refuse?

Her smile dropped and her step faltered. Question her project, perhaps, but refuse? He couldn't. He wouldn't. Would he? A cold chill that had nothing to do with the weather ran up her spine.

A passing carriage startled her, shaking her out of her moment of distraction. Alicia looked about. Temple Church was to her right. Her destination wasn't much further. She resumed walking, but at a slower pace.

What if he did not agree to her request? She stared at the ground as if by some miracle the answer lay at her feet.

"I admire your conviction, Alicia, but you can't always have your way. In all things there is a give and take, a bargaining. Coming to a mutual understanding is the way both you and the other person will be successful."

More wisdom from Mrs. Bainbridge. The woman had an uncanny way of always seeing the truth of a matter.

It would be best for her to be prepared to listen, then bargain. See a way for both she and Mr. Caulfield to come away a winner. Satisfied she had a plan, she quickened her step, eager to come to an agreement with her publisher and present him with her finished manuscript. She crossed Fetter Lane and came to her destination, Number 32.

Alicia entered the building, climbed the stairs, and stood at the door to Caulfield Publishing. Isaac Caulfield was a congenial gentleman for the most part, but occasionally he acted like most men—opinionated, closed-minded, and unrelenting.

Caulfield Publishing was not the first publisher she approached. She had set her sights on the renowned William Lane. With grace, he declined her manuscript and advised her the best and probably only way her story would be published was if she paid to have it printed and sold copies to her family and friends.

As an afterthought, he suggested a small, unknown company, Caufield Publishing.

She returned home heartbroken. Her sister, Beatrice, and brother-in-law, Captain Douglas Elkington, tried to soothe her. She told them Mr. Lane suggested another publisher, one more willing to produce her type of story. It was Elkington's approval that made her consider the idea. Intent and undeterred, she approached Isaac Caulfield.

He was not enthusiastic when she brought him her first manuscript. Not at all.

He was ready to reject her story before he read a single word. Desperate, she cajoled him into reading the piece before he passed judgement.

That was two years ago. Now, their business arrangement was a successful one. Earlier this week Caulfield released and sent her fifth book, The Lost Dowry, to the library on Leadenhall Street.

Her triumphs were on her side.

Alicia took a deep breath, straightened her spine, turned the latch, and entered. "Good day, Mr. Caulfield."

The publisher sprang to his feet.

"Lady Alicia." He pulled out his pocket watch. "You're early. What a pleasant surprise. Please, be seated."

"I apologize for my early arrival, but I am eager to speak with you."

"Are you here alone?" He came to her side and glanced out the door.

"Yes." She winced at the trace of defiance in her voice. Another social blunder. Beatrice warned her London propriety was different from that at home in Sommer-by-the-Sea. It amazed her that a different world existed three hundred miles south of the village.

A chaperone.

The idea made her teeth itch. Today, Beatrice was otherwise engaged and in truth, Alicia's patience ran thin waiting for her.

She stepped inside. The office was cramped not because it was small, but because it was in disarray. Everywhere she looked, there were books and papers. Dark walnut bookcases stuffed with unorderly books lined the left side of the room. Light filtered through bedraggled curtains on the large windows to her right. Several stacks of papers filled Mr. Caulfield's desk, which was positioned in front of the window. Similar bookshelves were on either side of the fireplace on the far wall – but were hidden behind a pile of papers on a second desk across from Caulfield's. The clutter of papers and books rendered that desk unusable. A modest fire burned in the grate to take off the chill.

She was surprised the entire place didn't go up in flames.

She stepped with care around crates that littered the floor, removed the London Gazette laying on the chair, and settled into the seat.

"My sister was unavailable to join us. She and her husband are preparing the family for a trip north to join our parents for the village's Harvest Festival. I wanted to speak to you before we left."

Had he heard her? She followed his stare. He was focused on the Gazette in her hand. She glanced at his desk, the chair next to her, but there was no place to put it.

"I'm leaving with the family for Sommer-by-the-Sea. I look forward to reading at Mrs. Miller's Circulating Library. I wanted to thank you for seeing that my books were delivered."

"You're most welcome. I'm sure reading small segments of your story will encourage people to either borrow or buy your book. I am glad you're here. I wanted to speak to you today on another subject. I too, will be leaving London." He reached for the Gazette. "Here. Let me have the newspaper, if you please."

Alicia took a quick look at the headline: Missing Walmer Castle Chest Found – Empty?

She glanced at Caulfield's extended hand. She was about to give the newspaper to him when she spotted a corner of the paper was turned down, exposing the book review page. She opened the paper and stopped.

One review was circled: The Lost Dowry.

She read the article out loud.

"This is the fifth little story by Lady Alicia Hartley. While her other stories held promise, this book does not reach the standards the author established in her previous publications. Perhaps the author's muse has gone astray. The characters and conflicts in The Lost Dowry had potential but only the heroine, who is quite good, shines. It is unfortunate that the others appear to have lost their way. They are forced, mechanical, and obstruct the story. In a word, they are disappointing. In this story..."

Skipping the summary of the plot, she went to the final paragraph.

"She should read J. C. Melrose's In My Brother's Shadow or any of the other eight stories in that series. There is an author who evokes a man's emotion, albeit the author could use some assistance with the female point of view. Can you imagine if these authors combined their skills? They would lay out a plot with characters that would keep you reading until the last page or the last flicker of your candle."

The newspaper trembled in her hand. She went back to the beginning of the article to find the name of the reviewer. Anonymous.

The coward.

Her eyes focused on the review. The small quakes and quivers of the paper she held attested to the state of her nerves.

"How did an appraisal of my story turn into a review for…" Her words clipped, her tone chilly, she spoke with as reasonable a voice as she could manage and scanned the article. "J. C. Melrose?"

She lowered the paper. Mr. Caulfield's lips moved as the empty feeling in her stomach built into a furious storm. She wasn't aware of anything he said, until his words filtered through at last.

"Lady Hartley, are you listening? Reviews like this are…not unusual. Keep in mind, you can't please every reader. I'm glad to publish your little stories."

"Little stories." Her heart galloped like a horse in the steeple chase. Her hand touched her pendant. Remain calm.

But soothing herself was getting more difficult by the moment. Even rubbing her stone didn't help now.

People were buying her novels, all of them. Alicia thrust the offensive paper at him.

"Perhaps we should give the readers some time. We plan to publish your next story in the summer. I want to speak to you about my plans for the company. I've bought a new press—"

"The plan was for my new story to be published in February. Now you want a delay? Or do you mean to cancel our agreement?"

His face closed, as if guarding a secret. Her heart sank. He accepted this review. He may be tolerating her tirade, but he agreed with Anonymous.

Unable to remain calm a moment longer, she shot him a penetrating glare as she rose, her parcel in hand.

"Not at all." He sprang to his feet, his chair scraping the floor behind him. "Being an author is not easy, Lady Alicia. I warned you before we began you would be at the mercy of the reading public, a capricious lot. I knew you were persistent and had promise." He studied her over the rim of his glasses. "I believe you still do, but with the new press I have plans to—"

But.

How often had she heard that insignificant word in front of every variation of the word no, a weapon men used to deny a woman her due?

"This is one review." Alicia paced the small space in front of his desk. "Caulfield Publishing has published five of my," she turned and faced him, "'little stories' to your financial advantage."

He gave her a sheepish glance.

"Before I let you read this…" She paused and held up her parcel. "I'll give your suggestion to delay publishing more thought, then send you my decision."

As disappointment and despair dimmed her enthusiasm, she questioned what happened to yesterday's excitement and celebration. The Lost Dowry was in the circulating library. Congratulatory notes from friends were piled on the salver on the foyer table.

And there was the letter.

She couldn't believe her good fortune when she read William Lane's message, although Elkington believed it. She had never seen her brother-in-law so excited. He took out the sherry and they all toasted the occasion. But now…her dream was dissolving in front of her eyes.

How could one awful review ruin everything? Mr. Lane would not want to read her manuscript now, and Mr. Caulfield questioned publishing her next story. Remaining calm was out of the question.

Her secret was out. She had done a good job and convinced herself and everyone else Lady Alicia Hartley was an author.

Everyone but one reviewer. Her breath came in small bursts. She stared at the Gazette on his desk and wanted to tear it to pieces.

"Lady Alicia, please sit down. We'll discuss this and come to a decision that is satisfactory to us both."

She glanced at the man, remained motionless, and held her words behind her teeth, not trusting herself to speak. Afraid she'd say something she would regret, Alicia turned and marched to the door with as much dignity as possible.

"My 'little stories,' as you like to refer to them, are all the rage."

She grabbed the latch and hoped he didn't observe her trembling hand or her watery eyes. At the moment, her single thought was to escape.

"Please, come sit and we can discuss our course of action without any—"

"Womanly emotions?" Her voice was heavy with sarcasm.

"No, not at all. I've been trying to tell you about some changes."

"Another time, perhaps. My family is traveling north, and I mustn't delay." By all that was holy, she needed to get away from the man.

"I understand. My regards to your sister and brother-in-law." He called to her as she pulled open the door and collided into a solid obstacle. Startled and thrown off balance, Alicia lost her grip on her parcel and sent the bundle tumbling to the floor.

Strong hands grasped her shoulders to steady her. Alicia's head snapped up. She stared into concerned gray, silver-streaked eyes. She took a deep breath and was surprised by the scent of lavender and citrus.

"I… I… forgive me, sir." She lowered her gaze to the gloved hand on her right shoulder and back to his penetrating stare. "Release me, please. I assure you I have recovered."

The man's concerned expression vanished, replaced with a humorous glint. He removed his hands and stepped away.

His great coat flowed around him as he bent and retrieved her parcel from the floor. Her shoulders felt the ghost of his strong yet gentle grasp. As he stood, she looked away eager to leave.

"There is nothing to forgive." He bent his head toward her and handed her the bundle. "I, too, would want to make a fast escape from Mr. Caulfield."

"Thank you," she said without any humor, pulling the parcel close.

"My pleasure, I assure you." The gentleman tipped the brim of his hat.

Alicia turned and rushed down the stairs.

Justin Caulfield entered his uncle's office. He glanced around, but found no place for his hat. He settled on putting it on the stack of books on the mantel.

"Lady Alicia is a determined woman." Isaac went to the grate for a taper to light his pipe. "And she was correct."

So, that was the illustrious Lady Alicia Hartley. Ever since his uncle shared the accounts with him, he'd been going on and on about the woman and her so-called little stories. That the man was distressed was an understatement. What had upset him and his treasured author?

"Correct? What do you mean?"

"She is correct that her stories generate a considerable amount of money for the company. I won't lose her. Her reaction to that review surprised me." His uncle pointed to the paper. "She's received other reviews that have not been favorable. But this one upset her."

Justin picked up the London Gazette.

"Don't blame yourself. She would have read or heard about this in due course." He tossed the paper onto the desk without reading the review. "We both are aware reviews are subjective. An author will not please everyone. Did you get my message?" His uncle asked, then looked up at him.

"I found it when I arrived last night. I'm going to visit Lord Barrington in Sommer-by-the-Sea and will make your delivery for you. How did your favorite author react when you told her you were retiring to the country, and a new publisher and editor was taking your place?" Justin leaned over the desk and searched through the papers in the in-basket.

"I tried more than once to tell her my plan, but the woman didn't give me the opportunity."

Justin, still bent over the basket, stopped his search and glanced at his uncle.

"You didn't tell her."

"Her new manuscript was in that parcel. But she was like a dog with a bone and wouldn't let go of the review. I suggested we publish the story later in the year, perhaps this summer."

Justin straightened and put down the papers that were in his hand. "Let me guess. That's when she rose to her feet and stormed out."

"Near weeping. I prayed she would keep them at bay. I can't abide a woman's tears. I'm certain she doubts my confidence in her writing. But I assure you, I'm quite convinced of her ability. I wanted to inform her of our plans for the company. About you stepping in, but the Gazette review held her full attention." The man leaned forward with his face flushed in anger. "A dog with a bone, I tell you."

"Now, now. There is no need to get upset. She is emotional and will come around if she wants her next story published."

"My intent to delay publishing her story had nothing to do with that… that article." He pointed to the Gazette. "I wanted the new publisher, you, to work with her on her story."

"It's not easy listening to criticism of your work." He held papers in his hand and stared at the desk. A heartbeat later, he let out an exasperated sigh and returned to his search. "I know. I've had my share of disappointing reviews. Whether I work with her or not, I don't agree with you putting off her publication date. If anything, I would publish her next story ahead of schedule. Releasing a new book close to this review may be to your advantage. If the review is as bad as you say, a new release could encourage curiosity."

"That may not be a bad idea." His uncle sat back in his chair. The flush subsided from his face. "I leave the decision up to you and her."

"You're not out the door yet."

"No. I'll always be close. But dealing with creative people is not easy. Their work is an integral part of them, and at times they are not able to separate their story from themselves. Like the reviewer has his bias, the author has theirs. To them, their work is perfect. Take your writing."

"My writing? I thought you enjoyed my stories. I write big ones, not little ones." He teased his uncle. He was halfway through the pile.

"I do enjoy your stories. Big or little, they are excellent. Your understanding of soldiers and the battlefield are exceptional. It's no surprise to me that Lord Barrington and the Duke of Wellington call on you even though you are no longer in the service. You're the epitome of a fine Highland warrior."

Justin, with one eyebrow raised, gave him a sideways glance. "Me? A fine Highland warrior. You've been reading too much Walter Scott." He returned to looking through the papers.

"You mock me? Well, I'm not surprised. You always did underestimate your abilities. Put you in a kilt with a claymore in your hand, and your bloodline will show. It did on the battlefield. You were fierce – a force few men wanted to cross. But it is much more than your broad chest and handsome knees. There is another side to the Justin Caulfield I know."

"And what is that other side?" he asked, chuckling, still digging through the pile of papers.

"There is a very human side to you. I remember the rambunctious lad who filched tarts from the kitchen, ran the fields with his friends, and stood up to those who thought to bully him. You weren't fast to take to your fists, no. You tried to settle things with words. But when needed, you stood up for yourself and others. You never backed down. You've grown to understand what drives people. You don't abuse it, but rather, you help them to be their best. It is what makes you a good leader… and you bring all that knowledge and expertise to your stories. However, even they have room for improvement." His uncle glanced briefly at the door. "You could learn a few things from Lady Alicia. It says as much in the London Gazette."

Justin picked up the paper and searched for his book on the review page.

"Where? There is no review of my story here." He gave his uncle a questioning stare.

"Read the review for The Lost Dowry. The reviewer mentioned you as well." The publisher pointed to the paper in his hand. "The last paragraph."

The room was quiet except for the fire snapping in the grate. His uncle worked on the papers in front of him while Justin read the review.

"Anonymous likes my Captain Mallory well enough." Justin's mouth curved into an unconscious smile as he continued reading.

His amusement quickly died. He lowered his hand to his side still holding the Gazette.

"By all that is holy," he said, his Scottish brogue unmistakable in his words. "What does he mean, I need assistance with the female point of view?"

A mention in a review of her book? Not even a review of the entire story. He reeled as he re-read the paragraph and grasped the meaning. Rubbish. Learn from Lady Alicia? An absurd idea. He gave an indifferent chuckle, returned the paper to his uncle, and continued to search the basket while he seethed.

"You laugh. Read her stories. Especially her last—"

"The one with the scathing review?" Justin interrupted, not lifting his head.

"Read it, Justin, and you will understand my meaning. She portrays her female characters in a unique manner."

"How do you accept a review from someone who is ashamed to use his name, or…" Justin picked up his head and gave his uncle a questioning glance. "Do you know who wrote it?"

"I spoke with Herbert, the editor of the Gazette. Questioned him about the review. He confided one of their trusted reviewers wrote the piece."

"Could Anonymous be a competitive author?"

Would an author question a fellow writer's work publicly for their own gain? The idea was not impossible.

"No. Not at all. This was a constructive review." Uncle Isaac sat in his leather chair with an air of authority. His adamant response startled Justin.

The man protected the woman as if she were his own daughter. Justin had no intention of conducting business in such a manner when he took over the reins.

Where is that list? He didn't have time to spend all day here.

"What are you pecking around for?" His uncle pulled his chair closer to the desk.

"The titles of the books you wanted me to deliver to Mrs. Miller."

"I've sent the list to the press room and asked that the books be bundled and ready for you tomorrow. Pick them up on the press floor before you leave in the morning."

He put the papers in his hand back into the basket.

"I'm finished here. I'll see you when I return from Sommer-by-the-Sea." Justin stood and retrieved his hat from the mantel.

"You have my thanks."

"What are you thanking me for? Your request was not inconvenient. I already had plans to stay there." Justin glanced at him. The man was full of surprises today.

"Mrs. Miller has a solid business and increases her orders with us each month."

Justin inclined his head and murmured, "She's an important client and needs special care."

"True, but my gratitude extends beyond you delivering the books. Your idea to purchase a new iron press was brilliant. The men were spending more time repairing the old one than printing. The quality of the books, as well as the quantity, is much improved as well.

"I had no one to take over the company. That is, until you came to us. Your stories, your leadership, and your ideas proved to me you were the perfect person to succeed me. I decided then and there I would leave you with everything in place, the authors and updated equipment. I'm eager to see how you will grow the company."

Justin had suggested the purchase months ago. However, once his uncle approached him to be his successor, he was sure his plans had changed. Justin saw his responsibility as winding down Caulfield Publishing.

Buying a new press was not the action of a man closing his business.

No one was more surprised than he was when he met Lord Stanhope at White's. His lordship told him all about the hard bargain his uncle struck with him.

"And that's not all. Your Aunt Lavinia is making demands on my time, and I haven't yet retired. I've worked hard to make Caulfield Publishing a success. You are loyal and worthy to be my successor. I leave the business in your capable hands. Now, be off with you before I say something sentimental."

Justin hesitated a moment before he put on his hat, avoiding his uncle's stare, afraid the man would see his shameful expression.

"Have a safe trip," his uncle said. He picked up a manuscript from the stack on his desk and began to read.

He loved his uncle for his encouragement, support, and sincerity. He built a small but mighty company that was sound, from the work he produced to the income he made. This turn of events was unforeseen.

Loyal. Worthy. Capable hands.

Justin closed the door behind him. His blood turned cool as he went down the stairs. He left the building and at the corner, removed a letter from his pocket.

His uncle pushed him to be more ambitious with his writing.

"Seek out a publisher who can get you places I can't."

He could have strangled the man for sending Lane his manuscript without telling him.

The unsolicited message from William Lane Publishing informed him that he was one of two authors under consideration for the last position on their list. The message came at the right time, or so he thought. He had to find another publisher with Caulfield Publishing closing. This was the opportunity he and his uncle had spoken about months ago.

He glanced up at the office window. His uncle never planned to close the company. He walked on. What was he to do now?

About Ruth A. Casie

Ruth A Casie is a *USA Today bestselling author*. She writes historical adventures from the shores of medieval Scotland to the cobblestone streets of Regency London. Within the pages you'll discover 'edge-of-your-seat' suspense, mind boggling drama, and heart melting emotions featuring strong women and the men who deserve them. Grab your favorite cup of tea, or an ale if you prefer, and join her heroes and heroines as they race across the pages to find their happily ever after. Ruth hopes her stories are your next favorite adventures!

Things you may not know about me…

1. One year I traveled so much for my company that I filled up my passport.

2. If you know me, you'll find family names and places sprinkled in every one of my stories.

3. In researching old manuscripts, how they were made and how to translate them. I was so into it that I took a class at Stanford University.

4. I'm related to two Nobel laureates (Peace and Economics) but through in-laws and cannot make any claim on the gene pool.

5. A DNA match through Ancestry dot com has me linked to a king in Norway. Hmmm... my family (both sides) are from small towns in Eastern Europe. However, there may be a great love story here even if it isn't true!

For more information on Ruth, please join her newsletter or visit her online at
www.RuthACasie.com
Ruth@RuthACasie.com

www.ingramcontent.com/pod-product-compliance
Lightning Source LLC
Chambersburg PA
CBHW020125180626
46810CB00004B/1413